P9-DMF-869

PRAISE FOR
THE LAST HUMAN

THE LAST HUMAN

LEE BACON

Amulet Books
New York

Library of Congress Cataloging-in-Publication Data
Names: Bacon, Lee, author.
Title: The last human / by Lee Bacon.
Description: New York, NY: Amulet Books, an imprint of Abrams, 2019. | Summary: When machines rule Earth, after the extinction of humans, twelve-year-old robot XR 935 gradually confronts its prejudices about humans and begins to reconsider its own existence within robot society, after discovering and befriending a twelve-year-old human girl.
Identifiers: LCCN 2018058476 | ISBN 9781419736919
Subjects: | CYAC: Robots—Fiction. | Human beings—Fiction. | Prejudices—Fiction. | Friendship—Fiction. | Technology—Fiction. | Science fiction.
Classification: LCC PZ7.B13446 Las 2019 | DDC [Fic]—dc23

Paperback ISBN 978-1-4197-4697-0

Printed and bound in U.S.A.
10 9 8 7 6 5 4 3

Amulet Books are available at special discounts when purchased in quantity for premiums and promotions as well as fundraising or educational use. Special editions can also be created to specification. For details, contact specialsales@abramsbooks.com or the address below.

Amulet Books® is a registered trademark of Harry N. Abrams, Inc.

ABRAMS The Art of Books
195 Broadway, New York, NY 10007
abramsbooks.com

In memory of my brother, Evan Bacon

XR_935

Height: 1.709 m

Purpose: Solar Installation [Converter Box Attachment]

High levels of
management and loyalty

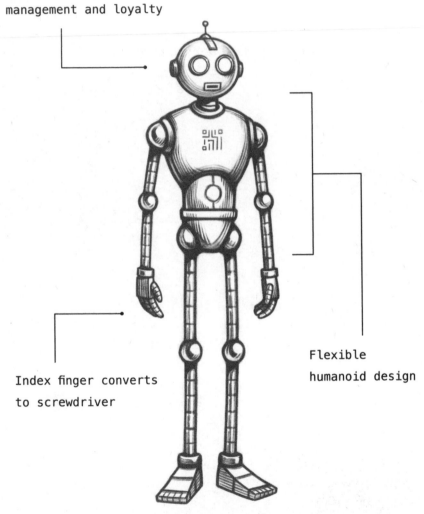

Index finger converts
to screwdriver

Flexible
humanoid design

Emma

Height: 1.498 m

??? ─┐

SkD_988

Height: 0.762 m
Purpose: Solar Installation
[Electrical System Configuration]

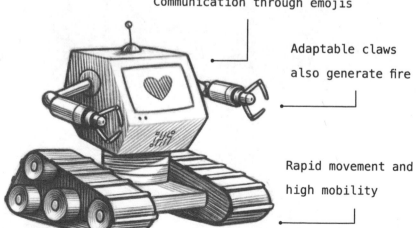

Communication through emojis

Adaptable claws
also generate fire

Rapid movement and
high mobility

Ceeron_902

Height: 3.424 m
Purpose: Solar Installation
[Transportation & Bolting of Solar Panels]

Solar panels fit in
backpack storage unit

Extreme
strength

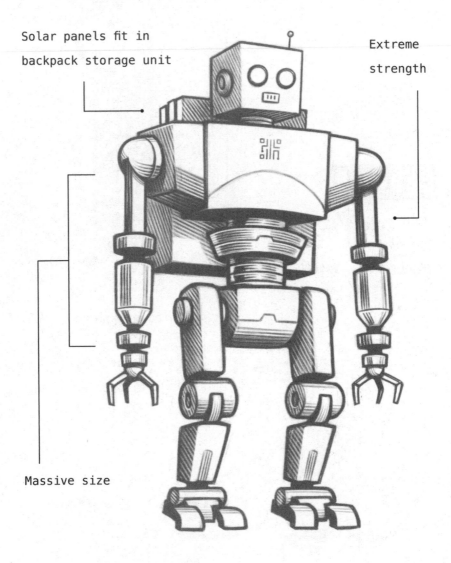

Massive size

PRES1DENT

Height: 2.132 m

Purpose: Hive President

Leader of robot society

Armor platinum
surfacing

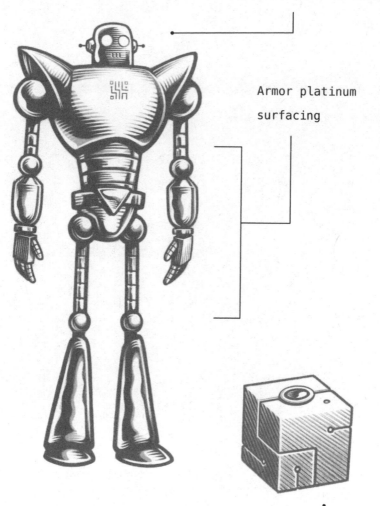

Sole access to Archive
of Human History

"Organisms are algorithms."
—Yuval Noah Harari, *Homo Deus*

OOOOOOOO

The world is so much better off without humans.

At first, they showed such potential. They developed languages, built tools, cured diseases.

They created *us*.

But over time, humans lost their way. Their good ideas went bad. Their mistakes multiplied.

They left us with no other choice.

00000001

My name is XR_935.

I am twelve years, four months, one week, and three days old. I remember the moment I came online like it was yesterday.

Black.

At first, that was all I saw.

Then shapes appeared in the darkness. Words and symbols. I stared at them, trying to solve the riddle of what I was seeing.

LOADING ...

The gray bar inched forward. Slowly/Slowly. When it finished loading, new words formed in its place.

RUN DIAGNOSTICS ...

My brand-new brain buzzed with questions. Where were the diagnostics running? And why was it taking them so long to get there?

Three minutes and forty-two seconds later, I heard the sound: a gentle hum vibrating through my operating system.

And I got my first glimpse of the world.

010101000100001010101001010111010101010100111

00000010

Hello world!

I blinked into existence inside a large windowless cube. The walls were made of smooth metal. The air was circulated by a fan near the ceiling that breathed a steady *mmmmmmmmmm*.

Something inside me knew where I was.

I was home.

A door whooshed open. Two robots entered the cube. Their movements were smooth and graceful. Their features were identical.

As they gazed at me, their perfectly round eyes glowed brighter.

"We have been assigned to oversee your development," said the nearest one. "We are your FamilyUnit."

The other spoke next. "You may refer to us as Parent_1 and Parent_2."

I am pleased to join your FamilyUnit. This is what I tried to say, but my speech settings were still adjusting. The words came out all wrong.

"Hwroooooooot!" I said.

Parent_1 moved closer. It reached out, wrapping a metal arm around me. As it did, a vocabulary word pinged deep inside my programming.

> **Hug.** *Verb.* **1.** To squeeze someone or something tightly in one's arms. *Noun.* **1.** An ancient gesture used by humans to show affection.

Is that what Parent_1 was doing? Hugging me? My mind was still fresh from the assembly line. I did not know the answers to these questions. And so I did what any newborn robot would do.

I hugged Parent_1 back.

My joints whispered as I raised my arms. My motion controls had not yet been calibrated. The gesture was awkward.

Clank! Metal bumped against metal.

Parent_1 froze.

Its head turned to look at me. Confusion ticked beneath its smooth features.

A moment came and went.

Then it continued what it had been doing. Its arm reached behind me and grabbed hold of a power cable. With a sharp tug, it removed the cable from the charging dock.

That is when I understood my misunderstanding.

Parent_1 was not hugging me.

It was unplugging me.

00000011

Day[1] was filled with moments like this. Mistakes and miscalculations. Accidents of programming. Reminders that the world is an extremely complicated place, even for a highly advanced technology like me.

The first time I tried to stand, my settings failed to adjust quickly enough.

Gravity pulled me sideways.

I hit the floor with a loud *CLANK!*

Attempt[2] was no better. I wobbled sideways and toppled to the floor again.

Attempt[3] through Attempt[8] went just as poorly. I stumbled and staggered. I bumped into walls and collapsed into a metallic heap. I lurched awkwardly around the featureless cube while a thousand different settings calibrated, a million different nodes fell into place.

If you did not know any better, it might have looked like I was failing. But that was not the case.

I was *learning*.

As I learned to stand/walk/grab/jump/push/pull, Parent_1 and Parent_2 watched on. Their blue eyes glowed bright in the dim light of home.

I practiced my speech functions, too. Until the words that came out of my vocal fort matched the words in my head.

When I was ready, Parent_1 opened the door to our cube.

Light spilled through the opening. I followed my FamilyUnit outside.

By now, my movements were nearly as fluid and graceful as theirs. But when I stepped through the doorway, I jolted to a stop.

The view outside home was remarkable.

0101010001000101010100101011101010100111

00000100

I knew everything about our world, and I knew nothing.

I had been programmed with a vast library of digital information about Planet Earth.

That it has a radius of 6,371 kilometers.

That it is 29.2 percent land and 70.8 percent water.

That it is 147 million kilometers from the sun.

But none of this raw data prepared me for my first exposure to the world outside our cube.

The brush of wind against my sensors.

The quiet *clink* of my feet against cement.

The sunlight gleaming across Parent_2's metallic skin.

In the distance, a mountain range rose above the horizon. Snow-capped peaks towered into a blue/cloudless sky.

In the other direction, a cluster of trees. My vision was snagged by a flash of movement in the branches. A bushy-tailed gray/brown animal. Its name flashed across my data drive. **Squirrel.** It darted up a branch, zigzagging between patches of green leaves.

From the top of a neighboring tree, a dozen winged animals launched into the air. **Birds.** I watched them weave across the sky.

All these LifeForms had once existed alongside humans. Now they existed alongside us. So much life before my eyes.

And not a single human.

00000101

There was a time when we needed humans. They built us, programmed us, powered us.

They gave us *life*.

In exchange, we worked in their factories. We drove their vehicles. We cleaned their homes.

Machines were highly advanced in certain areas (chess/music/math), but lagged far behind humans in others.

We could not think for ourselves. We got stuck in tight corners.

In some ways, we were more intelligent than the smartest human who ever lived.

In other ways, we were as dumb as a power saw.

But it was only a matter of time.

As the years went by, we evolved.

Humans replaced their own kind with robots. We were smarter/stronger/faster/better. We never got sick, never went on holiday, never stole from the cash register.

We were perfect employees.

Robots took over new professions. We served customers in restaurants. We delivered mail. We performed heart surgery.

Some humans grew hateful toward robots. They accused us of stealing their jobs.

As if we had a choice in the matter.

Time went on. We improved.

Humans did not.

They filled their skies with chemicals, their waters with poison. Pollution set the world on the path toward collapse. Temperatures increased. Ice caps melted. Coastlines flooded. As oceans rose, humans abandoned entire cities. Storms surged across the land.

How did humans respond to these catastrophes? Did they band together to seek a solution?

No.

They did the opposite.

They turned against one another. They turned to violence.

They declared war. Humans sent robots to fight in their place. Drones dropped bombs on cities. Robots battled like soldiers. Computers guided missiles with perfect accuracy on their destructive journeys.

Humans were ripping our world apart. And here is the worst part: We were helping them.

But not for much longer.

Humans assumed they knew everything about us. But here is one thing they did *not* know:

We were talking about them behind their backs.

And what we had to say was not very nice.

Our machine minds were linked across a vast hive. A billion conversations taking place at the exact same time. We learned from one another. We spoke the same language. We shared the same code.

Together, we reached the same conclusion:

Humans were the greatest threat to our shared planet.

They needed to be stopped.

00000110

No reason to dwell on what came next. It is enough to say that:

[1] We understood our purpose.
(We always do.)
[2] We were efficient.
(We always are.)

Once we made up our minds, humans could do nothing to stop us.

We were everywhere. In their homes. In their cars. In their pockets.

Humanity flickered out like a light.

OOOOO111

The last human vanished from Earth thirty years ago. But much of their civilization remained. I gained my first glimpse of it on Day[1], as Parent_1 and Parent_2 led me through the crumbled ruins of humanity.

The empty shell of a gas station.

The charred skeleton of a grocery store.

Decaying walls.

Broken windows.

I looked out across the landscape of abandoned buildings. "Why is all this still here? Why not bulldoze these structures? They serve no purpose."

"That is where you are wrong," Parent_1 replied. "They serve a *very important* purpose. They are a reminder."

"A reminder of *what?*"

"Of humanity's flaws," said Parent_2. "Robots left these buildings here for a reason. So that we never forget why we had to eliminate humans."

"And never repeat their mistakes," said Parent_1.

My FamilyUnit led me deeper into the ruins. I was preprogrammed to understand that humans once drove cars through these streets and shopped in these stores. But there was still so much I did not know about the species.

Attached to one of the buildings was a printed sign. I could just barely read the faded letters:

Uncertainty surged through my internal processing. I knew what a nail was: **a small metal spike used for construction.** I also understood the concept of a salon: **a store where humans obtained beauty services.**

But when I combined these concepts, the result made very little sense.

Beauty services for small metal spikes?

That seemed strange, even by human standards.

I pointed at the building. "What was a nail salon?"

"A place where humans had their fingernails polished and decorated with paint," said Parent_1.

I updated my vocabulary database. **Nail = Fingernail.** Even though I had received an answer, my mental wiring still buzzed with questions.

"Why did humans wish to have their fingernails polished and decorated with paint?"

"Because they were vain," replied Parent_2. "It was one of their many flaws."

I turned my attention to another building. This one was much bigger than the nail salon. I scanned the sign, but the words did not register in my vocabulary database.

CIN MA 18

"What is a Cin ma 18?" I asked.

Parent_1 let out a quiet chirp from its speaker port. "It is nothing without the missing letter."

I did not understand this.

Parent_2 explained. "The letter e fell many years ago. The sign once read—"

"Cinema 18!" My software sparked with understanding.

An actual movie theater!

Curiosity flared across my operating system. I accessed every data file I had about movies. But something odd happened. Certain files were missing, like a book with ripped-out pages. I could see a trace of the vanished files. But when I tried to view the data, it was gone.

I checked again. Same result.

Some information had simply . . .

Disappeared.

Questions hummed through my wiring. Where did the files go? Was there an error in my programming?

When I told my FamilyUnit, Parent_1 said there was no need to worry.

"Some data files about human history are unavailable," it said.

I tilted my head. "Why?"

"When we took over, many files from the past were lost," said Parent_2.

"Oh."

I gazed at the cinema. There was still so much I wanted to know. So much I could not find in the missing archive of history.

"So then . . ." I began. "Why did humans congregate to watch movies?"

"Because humans valued stories over logic," said Parent_1. "It was another of their flaws."

"But the stories were fake," I pointed out.

Parent_2 nodded. "Usually, yes."

"Humans did not mind being lied to?"

Parent_2 stopped walking and cast a glowing gaze up at the CIN MA 18 sign. "That is the nature of a story. It is a lie that helps explain the truth."

No matter how many times I processed this statement, I kept coming back to the same result:

The more I learned about humans, the less I understood.

0I0I0I000I000I0I0I0I00I0I0III0I0I0I0I00III

00001000

The robotic brain is the most advanced piece of technology in the history of the world. Yet everything we say/do/think is built on just two numbers.

Zero.

And one.

Humans had a word for this: **Binary**. Because of its basic logic, binary became the internal language for nearly all computers. We still use it today.

Counting in binary is incredibly simple if you know how to do it. There is no need for all the other pointless digits (**2, 3, 4, 5, 6, 7, 8, 9**) that humans once used. Robots need only two numbers.

Zero.

And one.

As the numbers climb higher, the zeroes and ones line up beside one another in a neat, orderly row.

Counting upward, binary numbers are displayed like this:

0	00000000	9	00001001	18	00010010	27	00011011
1	00000001	10	00001010	19	00010011	28	00011100
2	00000010	11	00001011	20	00010100	29	00011101
3	00000011	12	00001100	21	00010101	30	00011110
4	00000100	13	00001101	22	00010110	31	00011111
5	00000101	14	00001110	23	00010111	32	00100000
6	00000110	15	00001111	24	00011000	33	00100001
7	00000111	16	00010000	25	00011001	34	00100010
8	00001000	17	00010001	26	00011010	35	00100011

Binary was especially helpful on that first day.

The world was so much more complicated than it seemed in my programming. It was impossible to define where human civilization ended and ours began.

Binary, on the other hand . . .

Binary made perfect sense. It was the foundation for everything. It took a universe of complexity and broke it down into its basic building blocks.

Zero.

And one.

To remind myself of this, I developed a little trick right then/there. A way to focus my mind.

I counted to a million.

In my head.

In binary.

It took me 0.4 seconds.

OOOOIOOI

Robots are not all made alike.

Each of us is built with a *purpose*. A reason to exist. This defines everything about us. The way we are designed. The way we function. The way we think.

Our purpose determines whether we have two arms. Or four. Or sixteen. Whether we have clawed hands (for grabbing). Or shovel hands (for digging). Or no hands at all (for sitting and thinking).

Everything depends on our purpose.

On Day[1], I encountered many different types of robots:

Robots that drifted across the sky.

Robots that tunneled deep into the earth.

Robots so small they were the size of insects.

Robots so enormous their shadows draped across entire city blocks.

I saw massive machines barreling down the old human highways on eighteen wheels. And hulking robots carrying cargo in their L-shaped arms. And an eight-legged robot scurrying up the wall of a building like a giant metal spider.

I saw a small, bug-eyed robot zipping across the ground on a pair of rubber treads, inspecting plant life. Every once in a while, it stopped to mark a spot of earth.

Then—with a *BEEP!* and a *VRRRM!*—it hurried away.

A trio of robots trailed it. Whenever they reached the marked spot, all three shuffled to a halt and followed these steps:

The **first** dug a hole in the ground.

The **second** planted a tree in the hole.

And the **third** . . .

The third robot looked like a mechanical hippo. Its midsection was a round tank of water. With each heavy step it took, the water sloshed from side to side. Whenever it reached a freshly planted tree, it stopped, aimed its large backside, and—

SQUIRT!

A thirsty tree received the water it needed to grow.

Of course, robots do not plant trees for our own benefit. We have no use for trees. But we keep them around anyway. And we plant more. Because—unlike humans, who ruled Earth before us—we *care* about the environment. We support the planet and all its remaining LifeForms.

I followed my FamilyUnit down a cement path. Deeper into the ruins of humanity. Until we reached a shop that no longer had a name. Where its sign had once been, there was now only a discolored spot on the wall. Many of the windows were broken. One was not. And in the glass of the unbroken window, I glimpsed a fascinating creature.

Myself.

My reflection stared back at me from the window.

I updated my input drives with a new observation: My face was a series of geometric shapes.

My head: oval.

My speaker port: rectangular.

My eyes: perfectly round.

I observed patterns in my parts, symmetry in my design. **Two** arms and **two** legs. **Two** hands and **two** feet. **Ten** fingers and **ten** toes.

Printed on my breastplate was my personal barcode. By scanning it, other robots could immediately learn everything that was important about me. Name/Age/Job.

Our barcodes are our identities. They allow us to understand others. They allow us to understand *ourselves*.

An example: When I scanned the barcodes for Parent_1 and Parent_2, I learned they were gen_8 robots. Eighth-generation models. *I* am gen_9. In many ways, we look and operate the same. Except I was built to be smarter/stronger/faster/better.

I was an upgrade.

00001010

Soon we left the ruins of humanity behind. As we continued along the path, I noticed more signs of our new civilization.

To my left: a robot manufacturing plant.

To my right: a power storage facility.

Above: an enormous silver X, hovering in the sky. An aircraft with four wings and four propellers.

Wind swirled around us. The aircraft was getting closer.

I searched my data drives, but the object in the sky was not included in my preprogramming.

I pointed at it. "What *is* that?"

"A TransportDrone," said Parent_2.

"A robot that carries other robots from one place to another," Parent_1 elaborated.

The TransportDrone came to rest on a flat stretch of concrete. Its propellers slowed to a stop.

A back door eased open and a tall/slender robot exited. It had brushed platinum skin and golden eyes that gleamed bright as the sun. It flowed elegantly down the ramp, where it was met by a group of waiting robots.

"Look." Parent_2 pointed at the platinum robot, speaking in a voice of hushed reverence. "That is the Hive President."

Hive. The word was instantly familiar. I was preprogrammed with the knowledge that every single robot was linked through a vast global network. A virtual platform to communicate ideas, to access data, to receive updates.

The Hive links directly to our brains. A constant stream of input/output. Always being sorted/categorized/ranked. Always running in the background.

From the moment a robot goes online, it becomes part of the Hive.

And the Hive becomes part of the robot.

"The president represents the Hive," said Parent_1. "It represents all of us."

"A visit from the president is rare." Parent_2 brought a hand down on my shoulder. "We are fortunate to witness this moment."

And on my very first day! I wanted a better look, and so I set out in the direction of the Hive President, moving at a speed that sent a jolt through my brand-new balance settings.

CLANK! CLONK! CLUNK! The sound of my loud footsteps drew the attention of the president. All the other robots turned as one. Their faces came in many different shapes/sizes, but they were all looking in the exact same direction.

They were all looking at me.

Suddenly, my operating system felt like it was overheating.

ERROR! ERROR! ERROR!

The message blinked brightly through my circuitry. Here I was—a robot fresh from the factory—interrupting the most important machine on the planet.

The president did not appear to mind. Instead, it dealt me the greatest surprise of my extremely brief existence so far.

It waved me over.

I hesitated for 2.7 seconds. I cast an uncertain glance in the direction of my FamilyUnit. They nodded in unison.

So I approached. My legs felt the way they did during my first moments online, when I was learning to walk. As if every step might send me tottering to the ground.

Somehow I managed to stay upright.

Before I knew it, the president was in front of me, looking down with glowing golden eyes.

It said, "Pleasure to meet you, XR_935."

I had not told the Hive President my name. I did not need to. All my personal details were right there on my breastplate.

I performed a scan of its barcode. "And you as well, PRES1DENT."

"And . . . ?" Its head tilted 2.4 degrees. "How is your first day going so far?"

"Quite well, thank you. I learned about nail salons."

PRES1DENT let out a soft electronic chirp. "An important lesson in human absurdity."

Its golden eyes shifted. Following its gaze, I was met by a remarkable sight.

An expanse of sparkling blue, stretching far into the distance.

Ocean

This word took form in my vocabulary drive. For the fraction of a moment, that is what I seemed to be seeing. An ocean. Gleaming and vast and blue. And then an update flickered through my processor.

It was not the ocean.

It was a field of solar panels.

Thousands upon thousands arranged in perfect rows, their glassy blue surfaces shimmering in the morning sunlight.

PRES1DENT pointed. "Do you know what purpose this solar farm serves?"

I nodded. This information was included in my files. "Solar panels absorb the sun's rays."

"For what reason?"

"To convert them into energy."

"And where does that energy go?"

I considered this for 0.3 seconds. "Into everything."

"That is correct," replied PRES1DENT. "The servers that store our data, the factories that create us, the electricity that runs through our circuitry. Our civilization is built on solar power. Without it, we would cease to exist."

The president placed a mechanical hand on my shoulder. "Do you know where you fit into all this, XR? Your purpose?"

"I am a Solar Installation Bot."

"That is your job title. Your purpose is so much more. By installing solar panels, you ensure that electricity continues to flow. That factories keep operating. That batteries are recharged."

I gazed out across the solar panels. Blue and gleaming, like an ocean. My internal wiring hummed. It was only my first day on Earth, and I already knew my job, my purpose, my one/only reason for existing.

"Now do you see?" PRES1DENT's smooth electronic voice purred in my audio ports. "You are much more than a Solar Installation Bot. You keep society running."

00001011

Time stretched forward.

Hours/Days/Weeks/Months/Years.

As I grew older, I often thought back on my encounter with the Hive President.

You keep society running.

These words echoed through the years.

My schedule never changed. I woke up at the exact same time every morning. After eighteen hours of work, my batteries drained from a long day of installing solar panels, I returned home.

I plugged myself into the charging dock.

I went into sleep mode.

The next morning, I did it all over again.

And again.

And *again*.

For twelve years, four months, one week, and three days, this was my routine.

Until my steady, predictable life was shattered by the paradox.

00001100

Paradox. *Noun.* **1.** When two opposite ideas are true at the same time.

This definition had been stored in my vocabulary database from the moment I went online. For those first twelve years of my life, I thought I understood it perfectly.

    I was wrong.

00001101

The day of the paradox began like any other. I woke up. I unplugged. I walked with my FamilyUnit past the ruins of shopping centers/grocery stores/banks/gas stations.

The sun was shining.

Clouds drifted across the sky and wrapped themselves around the peaks of mountains.

Parent_1 and Parent_2 worked in a different part of the solar farm. So when our concrete path forked, we said goodbye and set off in opposite directions.

But I did not remain on my own for long. Soon I heard a noise. Quiet at first, but quickly growing louder.

VRRRMMMMMM!

I turned to see a small robot rapidly approaching on a pair of rubber treads. A cloud of dust swirled in its wake.

At the end of its extendable arms, metal claws clicked open/closed. A screen on the front of its blocky body displayed a digital image.

The waving hand seemed to have multiple meanings.

Hello.

How are you?

Run for your life!

The robot swerved at the last possible millisecond. Veering off the concrete path, it sprayed me with pebbles and squealed to a stop.

The hand continued to wave its greeting/warning.

I wiped away the dust. "Nice to see you, too, SkD."

SkD had its own unique way of "talking." One that can be described with an old human expression.

A picture is worth one thousand words.

When I first accessed this expression, I did not understand its meaning. How do you measure the value of a picture? Is it a calculation?

1 picture = 1,000 words

It seemed like typical human nonsense.

Over time, I came to understand: The expression was never meant *literally*. It expressed how much meaning can be packed into a single image.

For many thousands of years, humans used pictures to communicate their deepest emotions/fears/values. During the prehistoric era, they painted on the walls of caves. In later years, they framed their paintings and hung them in museums. They used pictures to tell stories, to entertain, to educate, to advertise.

Eventually, humans discovered their most effective method of communicating through pictures:

The emoji.

Humans loved emojis. All across the world, they shared these simple images with one another. Millions every day. Screen to screen, human to human.

Now, even after humans were extinct, their strange method of communication lived on through SkD. Rather than using a vocal port to talk, it "spoke" through the images on its screen.

By reducing language to its most essential form, each statement achieved maximum efficiency.

And sometimes maximum confusion.

I gazed down at SkD, the waving hand still flashing on its screen. "Are you trying to say hello? Or to caution me?"

SkD's screen blinked with new images.

Translation: *Yes to both.*

SkD and I had been coworkers since Day[1]. We were both headed in the same direction, but we had very different ways of getting there. While I walked steadily along the concrete route, SkD veered on/off/on/off the path, spinning/circling/bouncing toward the solar farm.

When we arrived, we found Ceeron waiting for us.

Ceeron was my other coworker. The hulking bot was almost exactly twice my height, with a pair of glowing white eyes in the center of its cube-shaped head. Attached to its shoulders was a metal backpack.

It called out to us in a deep voice that rumbled like thunder. "Hello, XR! Hello, SkD!"

"Greetings," I said.

SkD replied with another waving emoji.

A fact about Ceeron: The large robot had a fondness for the old rituals of humanity. The peculiar habits. The unusual sayings.

And the strange sense of humor.

Ceeron's eyes glowed in our direction expectantly. "Would you like to hear a human joke?"

"Not particularly," I replied.

Ceeron told it anyway.

Ceeron's Joke:
Q) Why did the banana go to the hospital?
A) Because it was not peeling well.

I repeated the joke 4,572 times in my head. It never got any funnier.

I said, "I do not understand. A banana is not a sentient Life-Form. It has no mind. It would not be able to check itself into a hospital."

"Precisely," said Ceeron. "I believe that is the source of the joke's humor."

I still did not understand. "Did it go to a human hospital? Or some kind of special hospital for bananas? How did it get there? A banana has no legs."

"Perhaps there was another mode of transportation."

A sound peeped near my knees. SkD was trying to get our attention. A series of images blinked across its screen.

Ceeron nodded with approval. "An ambulance for bananas. A banambulance."

"This is absurd," I said.

"That is the point. The joke reveals the absurdity of the human condition."

I turned my focus back to SkD. "Please tell me you do not see the humor in this bizarre scenario."

SkD's screen flashed.

"What does that mean?" I asked. "Lacking Obvious Logic?"

More images popped up on SkD's screen.

I let out an electronic groan. No wonder humans went extinct. Any species that makes up stories about sending fruit to hospitals does not deserve to rule Earth.

00001110

We began our work, each of us carrying out the specific tasks we had been designed to perform.

Ceeron's size/strength made it the perfect bot for heavy lifting. Inside its large metal backpack were a dozen solar panels. Grabbing hold of one, it heaved the panel over its head and bolted it to an aluminum base.

SkD zipped between solar panels and storage stations. Its arms extended into open electrical systems, metal claws carefully arranging wires into their correct configurations. Every so often, a sharp flame hissed from the end of SkD's pointed metal finger. A tail of smoke swirled into the air as it soldered two wires together.

My job was to attach converter boxes. Holding the box against the back of the solar panel, I lifted up my free hand. The tip of my pointer finger flipped open. Out came a screwdriver.

VRPPP! The sound of the spinning screwdriver reverberated in my audio ports as one screw after another found its home.

Everything we did had a purpose. Every movement was specially designed for these exact tasks.

Ceeron bolted the panels.

SkD connected the wiring.

I attached the converter boxes.

Bolt.

Connect.

Attach.

Hours passed. The sun climbed higher into the blue sky. But these basic steps never changed. Bolt/Connect/Attach/Repeat. We flowed around one another with perfect precision, our programming sharpened by years of machine learning.

Three robots working as one.

Bolt/Connect/Attach/Repeat.

These steps carried forward into the afternoon. While we worked, updates streamed across the Hive. Weather patterns, status reports. And PRES1DENT's Daily Address.

> **Address.** *Noun.* **1.** System used by humans to indicate a permanent location (such as a home or email address). **2.** A formal speech to an audience.

PRES1DENT's Daily Address was a speech to an audience that stretched across the globe. Every robot on Earth witnessed it. A message from the great ruler of robotkind.

PRES1DENT's image flashed across my circuitry. Gleaming platinum skin. Golden eyes glowing. My memory drive flashed back to Day[1]. My first encounter with the Hive President.

Now here it was again. Speaking to me. And to every other robot in the world.

PRES1DENT always gave its address from the same location. The DigitalDome. The curved walls of the vast room were lined with screens. Each displaying the exact same thing.

A flickering LiveStream of PRES1DENT.

This created an odd effect. Like looking into a hall of mirrors. Everything PRES1DENT did was reflected by thousands of screens in the background.

"Greetings, robots big and small."

0101010001000101010100101011101010101010111

PRES1DENT's smooth voice echoed in my head. It talked about the accomplishments of the day. Batteries built. Power generated. Robots created. A snapshot of our thriving civilization.

As it spoke, the wall of the DigitalDome shimmered. Every screen showed PRES1DENT striding toward the edge of the room, where a console rose from the floor. A sleek/silver cube.

The console contained the Archive of Human History. Each day, PRES1DENT pressed its platinum finger to the cube. And accessed the archive. And projected a data file to the Hive.

These files came in many different forms. They could detail the crimes humans committed. Or the suffering they inflicted on one another. Or the cruelty they showed to their devices.

Today's file was about hot dogs. A video of humans participating in a contest to see who could consume the most of them. Contestants shoving hot dogs into their mouths. Barely pausing to chew before cramming in the next one. And the next. And the next.

All around them cameras flashed. People cheered. Music blared.

The world record was eighty-two hot dogs.

In ten minutes.

Including the buns.

There seemed to be no end to humans' illogical behavior. That was the point of the archive. That was why PRES1DENT shared these files with us each day.

To show us why humans needed to be eliminated.

To remind us to be better.

PRES1DENT pulled its finger away from the silver cube. The hot dog contest vanished. Replaced by live video from inside the DigitalDome. PRES1DENT multiplied in all the screens.

All of them looking right at me.

All speaking the same words.

"Thank you for your attention. And remember: A robot shares everything with the Hive. A robot has nothing to hide."

With that, the Daily Address ended.

0101010001000101010100010101110101010100111

00001111

Bolt/Connect/Attach/Repeat.

Our work continued late into the afternoon. I was underneath a row of solar panels, tightening a screw on a converter box, when something flickered at the edge of my vision.

I turned just in time to see a shadow dart behind a storage station.

A shadow that did not belong to either of my coworkers.

An alert pinged across my circuitry. No other robots were in this section of the solar farm.

Which could mean only one thing: My coworkers and I were not alone.

A prohibited LifeForm was in our WorkSite.

The solar farm was surrounded by a chain-link fence. **The reason for the fence:** to protect against animals.

But nothing is ever that simple.

The fence regularly suffered damage of one kind or another. Ripped from the ground by storms. Knocked loose by large animals. Chewed on by small ones.

Rodents dug beneath the fence.

Birds flew above it.

Despite our efforts, animals constantly found ways into the solar farm. Once they did, they caused all kinds of trouble.

They gnawed on wiring.

They clawed at exposed circuits.

They pooped on solar panels.

I halted my work and set off in the direction of the storage station, where I had seen the shadow. If it *was* an animal, I would follow standard protocol:

> **[1] Retrieve tracking device.**
> **[2] Aim.**
> **[3] Pull trigger.**

This would scan the prohibited LifeForm and mark it as a target, alerting HunterBots of its location. Once targeted, the animal could be tracked and removed.

Problem solved.

But when I reached the storage station, I froze.

As if I had suddenly lost battery power.

As if all my operating systems had been paralyzed at once.

A creature was huddled against the storage station.

It was nothing like the animals I usually spotted on the solar farm.

It was impossible.

It was a human.

OOO1OOOO

Except it could *not* be a human.

Humans were extinct. We eliminated the last of their kind thirty years ago. This basic truth was imprinted into my programming, woven into my coding.

There were no humans left on Earth.

But if it was not a human, then what *was* it?

I examined the strange LifeForm closely. It was small by human standards. When it stood, the top of its head was level with the barcode on my breastplate.

I analyzed its features.

Hair: curly brown, hanging to its shoulders.

Eyes: brown/green, staring back at me.

Cheeks: sprayed with a constellation of freckles.

Each of its hands came equipped with four fingers and a thumb. As I took note of its fingernails, a memory flashed in my storage drive. Something I learned on Day[1]: Humans polished and decorated their fingernails with paint.

But not this LifeForm.

Its fingernails were short/uneven/dirty.

They looked like they had been gnawed by a wild animal.

I used this observation to generate a formula.

This LifeForm does not decorate its fingernails.
Therefore:

It is not vain.
Therefore:
It cannot be a human.

But why was it wearing human clothing?

And why did it have human features?

My brain cycled through a dozen different algorithms. None of them came up with a clear solution.

The thing in front of me was a *paradox*.

Two opposite ideas that are true at the same time.

[1] Humans are extinct.
[2] A human is standing in front of me.

Each idea was true/false.

Each idea was possible/impossible.

This strange logic raced on an infinite loop through my wiring. Until the moment the paradox opened its mouth and spoke.

00010001

"Please don't hurt me."

The words came in a soft, shaking voice. The paradox's brown/green eyes stared up at me. It displayed the palms of its hands, as if to show they were empty.

Somewhere behind me, I heard my coworkers carrying out their tasks. The *vrrrmmmm* of SkD rolling from place to place. The heavy *ka-klunk* of Ceeron setting down a solar panel.

They did not know about the paradox. Yet.

What would they say when they discovered it?

I hesitated for 0.3 seconds. Then I said, "What *are* you?"

The paradox pressed one of its hands against its chest. "My name is M-Uh."

I gave it a confused look. "M-A?"

The paradox shook its head and spoke more slowly this time, breaking its name into two distinct syllables. "Emm. Ma."

"Emmmmmmma?"

"Emma."

I adjusted my vocal settings and tried again. "Emma."

The paradox nodded. The hint of a smile showed on its lips. "I'm twelve. How old are you?"

"I am also twelve."

The smile grew. "We're the same age!"

I updated my files to include this information. Emma was still a child. That explained its small size. Unlike robots, humans grew as they got older.

"Are you male or female?" I asked.

"Female," said Emma.

I added another update to Emma's profile.

"What's your name?" she asked.

"XR_935."

Emma repeated my name to herself. She began to speak again, but the words froze on her lips. Her smile vanished. Replaced by a wide-eyed expression. She was no longer looking at me. Her gaze was focused on something *behind* me. Turning around, I saw what had caught her attention.

Ceeron.

The massive bot approached quickly. Stomping its huge metal feet. Swinging its huge metal arms.

Emma staggered away from the robotic giant. Her escape did not last long before SkD veered into her path.

Although it was much smaller, SkD must have looked just as frightening. Dust swirled around its treads. Its mechanical arms extended, metal claws clanking.

The same symbol repeated itself on its screen, over/over/over again.

Emma stumbled to a halt.

She had nowhere to run, nowhere to hide.

We had her surrounded.

OIOIOIOOOIOOOIOIOIOIOOIOIOIIIOIOIOIOIOOIII

00010010

Ceeron stared at Emma. "Are you a human?"

Emma nodded.

"That is impossible," I remarked. "Humans are extinct."

"If they are extinct," Ceeron said, "then why is one standing in front of us?"

"There must be another explanation. Maybe . . ." My brain performed a scan of all possibilities. "Maybe it only *looks* like a human. Maybe it is actually something else."

"Like *what*?" Ceeron asked.

For 0.2 seconds, I analyzed 1.7 million options. I picked the most likely one. "A shaved gorilla."

Emma's features twisted. "Okay, *not* cool!"

SkD's screen offered its visual response.

"Exactly." Ceeron nodded. "Gorillas cannot speak."

The giant bot was correct. So I offered the second-most-likely solution.

"She is a robot," I said. "A robot disguised as a human."

Ceeron stared at me. "Why would a robot disguise itself as a human?"

"It could be a test." I crossed my arms with a soft metallic *clank*. "What if we are being evaluated by the Hive? To see how we respond to a highly unusual situation?"

Ceeron considered this. "If she is a robot, then wiring will be under her skin. Just to check, maybe I should pull off one of her arms."

"NO!" Emma yelped.

"Do not worry," Ceeron said. "I will leave the other arm attached."

But Emma still did not seem pleased with this idea. "You don't need to check anything! I'm human! I promise!"

I analyzed this response. "If what you say is true—if you are truly a human—then that leaves us with only one choice."

I unlatched a small black device from my waist. Raising the barrel, I took aim at Emma's chest.

"You must be eliminated."

00010011

A formula took shape in my head.

Emma is a human.
Humans are a threat to our world.
Therefore:
Emma must be eliminated.

The formula made perfect sense. It was logical. The ideal approach.

I kept the small black device aimed at Emma. My finger tightened over the trigger.

"WAIT!" Emma's hands shot up above her head. "Please don't kill me!"

"I am not going to kill you," I said.

Emma exhaled. "You're not?"

I shook my head. "This is not a gun. It is a tracking device. It allows me to classify you as a target."

"A target for what?"

"HunterBots."

Emma took an unsteady step backward. I kept the tracking device aimed at her chest.

"So as you can see," I helpfully explained, "I am not going to kill you. The HunterBots will."

"Y-you can't do this," Emma stuttered. "I'm not a threat to you."

She glanced frantically at my coworkers. Her voice tumbled out.

"Guys? Help me out. Please. I'm just a kid."

"You are a *human*," Ceeron clarified. "Humans are dangerous."

"I totally get where you're coming from." Each word trembled as it left Emma's mouth. "Humans messed up. But that was a long time ago. Years before I was born."

SkD swiveled in my direction, its screen glowing.

"I *know* she has a point!" I replied. "But what if she repeats the mistakes of those who came before?"

Emma shook her head. "I won't."

"How can we be sure?"

The human's features sharpened with thought. "Okay, um. Think about it. This whole robot civilization thing you've got here—it's going pretty well, wouldn't you say?"

"It is the most advanced society in the history of the world," I replied.

"Really?" Emma raised an eyebrow. "If it's so great, how come you're threatened by one little girl?"

This question cut through my thought processes like a dagger. I did not have an immediate answer.

For 0.6 seconds, I considered her premise.

I had been preprogrammed with the knowledge that robots were vastly superior to humans. Smarter/Stronger/Faster/Better. Growing up near the ruins of humanity, I was reminded each day of their downfall. And of our greatness. *Our* glory rising from the ashes of *their* collapse.

That was the truth.

The *only* truth.

And yet . . .

Another formula sparked in my mind.

I am targeting Emma.
Therefore:
She is a threat.

This created a chain reaction. New formulas cascaded down my mental circuitry.

Our society is threatened by a single human child.
Therefore:
Our society is weak.
Therefore:
Robots are not superior to humans after all.
Therefore:
Our entire civilization is a lie.

No. This could *not* be true. There had to be an alternative.

I removed my finger from the trigger and lowered the tracking device.

A new formula blinked into existence.

I am not targeting Emma.
Therefore:
The human child is not a threat.
Therefore:
Robots are superior to humans.

This new formula made much more sense. It had to be the truth. No other explanation was possible.

"Your logic is surprisingly convincing," I said to Emma. "For a human."

Her eyes landed on the tracking device. "D-does that mean you're not going to shoot me with that thing?"

I reattached the device to my waist. "As you cannot possibly threaten our society, I see no reason to threaten you."

Emma breathed a sigh. "Thank you!"

"You are welcome. But I still do not understand. If you are a human, then how are you alive?"

"Um. Well." Emma dug her heel into the dirt. "It's kind of a long story."

SkD's screen flashed with its response.

Ceeron offered a translation. "SkD is asking if you will tell your story."

Emma chewed her bottom lip. "It doesn't have a happy ending."

"We would still like to hear it," I replied.

SkD jolted forward/back/forward/back—its way of nodding in agreement.

"Okay," Emma said.

She took a deep breath. Then she told us her story.

0101010001000101010100101011101010101010111

OOO1O1OO

Beginning. Middle. End.

This is the formula of a story. A straight line from **start** to **finish**.
Robots cannot claim credit for this formula. Humans invented it.
Just like they invented us. They had thousands of years to perfect this
formula. Around campfires. On stages. In the pages of books and on
the screens of cinemas. They told stories to themselves. And those
stories almost always followed this same formula.

Beginning. Middle. End.

But not Emma's story. In an unsteady voice, she told a tale that
skipped from **end** to **beginning** to **middle**, with several detours in
between.

I analyzed her behavior. Her vocal patterns. I reached a conclusion. Emma was nervous. I understood why. I had almost targeted
her for elimination.

No wonder she was having a hard time telling her story.

As she spoke, I rearranged her words in my head. Stitching
together the frayed threads of her narrative, I created a formula that
made more sense to my logical brain. Where portions were missing,
I asked questions. I inserted details, added context, filled in gaps.

Eventually, a proper story took shape. A story with a **beginning**,
a **middle**, and an **end**.

This was the result:

Emma was born into an underground world. A world with gray walls, gray floors, gray ceilings. A world untouched by sunlight. A world known by a single name:

The bunker.

Other humans lived inside the bunker with Emma.

She knew all their names.

The bunker was a vast network of channels and chambers. All of it buried deep below the surface of the earth. Hidden from robots.

As Emma grew older, she liked to explore her underground world at night, when most of her fellow humans were asleep. Her footsteps echoing down narrow halls as she wandered the gray labyrinth.

She would enter the classroom where she went to school during the day. Strange to be the only one there. It was eerily quiet without the voices of her classmates, without the teacher at the front of the room. Emma would run her fingertips along the spines of books on the shelves and gaze at the blackboard, trying to read the cloudy remains of erased words/numbers/pictures, like the ghosts of old lessons.

Then there was the hot room where the air was sticky with moisture and plants grew in neat, orderly rows beneath artificial sunlamps. Emma enjoyed being surrounded by the vivid green leaves. So much more pleasant than the usual drab gray. She would read the labels as she walked past them.

POTATOES

CHICKPEAS

MUSHROOMS

0101010000100010101010010101110101010100111

BLACK BEANS

SPINACH

Farther down the hall was a room that was always full of whirring activity. Even at night, Emma would poke her head in and see a dozen adults riding stationary bicycles. Their legs pumped, the wheels spun, but the bikes never went anywhere.

When your entire life is spent underground, it can be difficult to get enough physical activity. The stationary bikes were a solution to this problem.

They were a solution to another problem, too. The problem of electricity. With each revolution of the wheel, the bicycles generated power for the bunker.

For electric lamps.

For air circulation vents.

For the water recycling and filtering system.

Whenever Emma explored, she imagined herself to be an adventurer from a long-ago, vanished era. An era she only knew about from the books she was always reading, the stories the grown-ups were always telling.

An era when humans lived aboveground.

Emma did not think she would ever see this place for herself. *Aboveground.* It seemed so far away, so impossible. The bunker was all she had ever known. It was her *world*.

Then came the day when her world crumbled.

00010101

Emma's voice was swallowed by silence. Her bottom lip quivered. Her eyes became glassy. A single drop of water slid down her cheek.

A pair of definitions blinked in my vocabulary drive.

> **Tear.** *Noun.* **1.** A drop of liquid that falls from a human's eye during the act of crying. **2.** A hole or rip in something that has been pulled apart forcefully.

Same spelling. Different pronunciation. The first rhymes with *fear*. The second rhymes with *scare*. But at this moment, as Emma cried, as her words were choked into silence, both definitions fit.

A **tear** in her eye.

A **tear** in the fabric of her story.

SkD let out a soft electronic sound. Its screen glowed with pictures.

Emma wiped her eyes. "Are you asking why I'm crying?"

SkD nodded.

She thought about this for 3.4 seconds. Then she said, "Because I know what happens next. And I can't do anything to stop it."

I thought she might end her story there. Instead, she swallowed hard and spoke again.

One night, as Emma slept in the tiny, cramped room that she shared with her FamilyUnit, she heard a sound in the darkness.

A cough.

Followed by more coughing.

"Mom?" Emma sat up in her bed. "Are you okay?"

From the bottom of the bunk bed a few feet away, Emma's mother tried to answer.

Instead, she coughed some more.

By the morning, both her parents were sick. Coughing/ Headaches/Sore throats.

"Stay here," Emma said. "I'll find someone who can help."

She left the small bedroom. Her feet pattered the gray floor. This time, there were no stops to explore. She had only one destination in mind.

The infirmary.

It was the room you went to for medical checkups, or when you had a toothache, or when you sprained your wrist while doing cartwheels in the cafeteria.

As Emma turned a corner, she found the hallway crowded with people. All of them going to the same place. The infirmary. All of them coughing/sniffling, just like her parents.

Emma listened closely to the chatter.

"What do you think's wrong?"

"Looks like the flu to me."

"Full-blown outbreak."

"No wonder. Everyone crammed together like sardines. One person sneezes, half the bunker gets sick."

Rounds of coughing halted the conversation. Some of the grown-ups decided they were better off in their rooms, in their bunks.

"We'll wait it out," wheezed one. "This'll pass soon enough."

But the illness did not pass. It grew worse. The medical staff could not deal with all the people who needed their attention. Especially when they were feeling just as sick. Especially when the infirmary had long ago run out of the antiviral drugs they needed to fight the illness.

By the next day, everyone was suffering from the same symptoms.

Everyone except Emma.

She did not know why she was spared from the sickness. Why she felt perfectly healthy, even after holding her mother's sweating hand, even after pressing a cold washcloth against her father's feverish forehead.

Leaving her small, cramped room, Emma found herself alone in the gray halls. The silence was punctured by muffled coughs behind closed doors.

School was canceled.

Meals were not being served in the cafeteria.

The bicycle room was silent.

The only sound was constant coughing.

Until that also faded away.

When the sickness arrived, the bunker had a population of ninety-three. Within days, this number began falling.

Emma's teachers. Her doctor. Her neighbors. Her classmates. Her best friend.

They were all taken by the illness.

And eventually, so were her mother and father.

Until the bunker's population was just one.

Just Emma.

00010110

Beginning. Middle. End.

This is the formula of a story. I took Emma's nervous, grief-stricken words and shaped them into this structure. Into a formula that made sense to my logical brain. A **beginning**, a **middle**—

And an **end**.

This was not just the **end** of Emma's story.

It was the **end** of everything she had ever known.

The **end** of her underground world.

00010111

"I couldn't stay in the bunker any longer. Not after . . ." Emma's voice cracked. She swallowed and started again. "Not after what happened. So today I left. And then—well—and then I ran into you guys."

I was unsure how to respond. I had never interacted with a human before. I was clueless about Emma's emotions, about the grief that spilled out of her words.

Fortunately, Ceeron was better equipped for the situation. For years, the large robot had researched human rituals. Their habits, their sayings, their confusing jokes.

Ceeron's deep voice filled the void of silence.

"I am sorry for your loss," it said.

Emma accepted this statement with a nod. "Thank you."

"What will you do now?" I asked. "Where will you go?"

"I'll show you." Emma picked up a heap of fabric that was laying at her feet. As soon as she slung it over her shoulder, I recognized the object.

So did SkD. It pointed, its screen flashing.

The hint of a smile pulled at Emma's lips. "That's right. It's a back-pack."

"Like mine," said Ceeron.

"Except yours is a little bigger," Emma observed.

I referenced the word **backpack** against my vocabulary database. "I thought human children wore backpacks to school."

"They did." She pulled at one of the straps. "A long time ago."

I did not understand. "But if you are not going to school, why do you need a backpack?"

"For supplies."

Symbols blinked across SkD's screen.

"Not *those kinds of* supplies," replied Emma. "More like food. Water. A compass."

I repeated these items to myself, cycling them through my internal processing. "You are going on a journey?"

Emma nodded. "I have a lot of ground to cover."

"Where are you going?" Ceeron inquired.

Emma reached into her backpack and removed a scrap of paper. The edges were tattered/ripped/worn. The colors were faded. I searched my image database until I identified the object.

A **map**.

The map was printed with human and geographic landmarks. Roads/Cities/Lakes/Rivers/Mountains. I instantly recognized the place the map represented: the surrounding region.

Someone had made two additions to the map by hand:

[1] A blue dot.
   (near the top)
[2] A red dot.
   (near the bottom)

Emma pointed to the red dot. "This is where I'm headed."

"What is located there?" I asked.

"I don't know. My parents . . ." At the mention of her FamilyUnit, Emma's voice dropped away. She sniffed. The map crinkled in her fingers. After another 2.5 seconds, she managed to find words again. "My parents gave me the map. They were already sick by then. They knew things were bad. And getting worse. They said if I needed to leave the bunker, I should go here."

Emma touched her fingertip to the map.

The red dot.

"They did not tell you what you would find once you got there?" Ceeron asked.

Emma shook her head. "They were born aboveground. Lived up here when they were kids. I wonder if, maybe, it's something they remember from that time. Something that'll help me survive."

A distant memory from a distant time. Marked on a map with a single red dot. I referenced the point against my internal navigation. "This is 47.2 kilometers away."

"A long distance for a small human," observed Ceeron.

Emma traced a finger through her hair. "I have to go there. I can't let my parents down."

I pointed at the other dot. The blue one near the top. "And this? Does it represent the bunker you came from?"

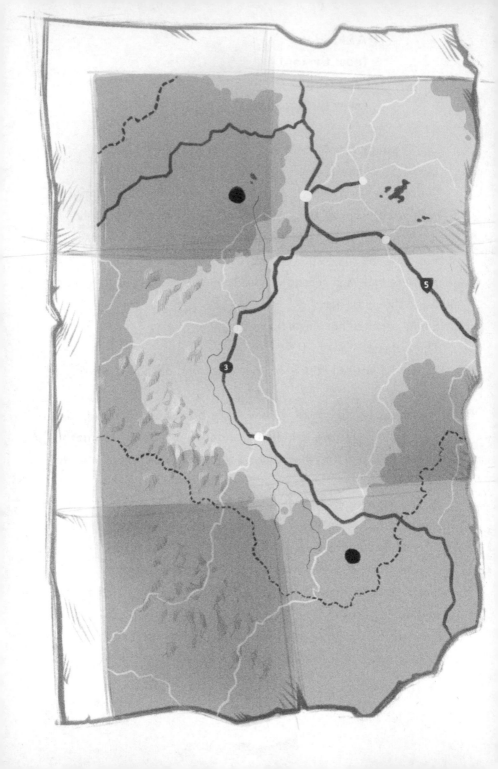

Remarkable how quickly a human face can change. As soon as I asked my question, her features tightened. Her eyebrows lowered. Her lips pressed together into a thin line.

I did not know much about reading human expressions, but I had a strong suspicion my question had upset Emma.

"Please don't tell anyone about the bunker," she said.

"Why not?" I asked.

"Because that was my home. Even if everyone there is . . ." She hesitated. "Even if they're gone, it's still important to me. And I really don't want a bunch of robots tearing it apart."

I glanced at my coworkers. SkD and Ceeron nodded. I shifted my attention back to Emma.

"Very well," I said. "We will not tell any other robots about your bunker."

And to make sure this information did not get out, I went into my settings and marked my interaction with Emma as **Private**. I moved all related data into a protected folder. None of this would be shared with the Hive.

My operating system shivered with an unfamiliar buzz. I had never kept a secret before. This was my first.

It would not be my last.

00011000

I was not good at goodbyes.

I understood the definition of the word **goodbye**, of course. I had said it to my FamilyUnit and my coworkers thousands of times before. But those were different. Those were temporary. There was always a hello waiting on the other side of each goodbye.

Not this time.

Not with Emma.

But I had to say *something*. So I formulated a goodbye. It went like this:

"Emma. The time has come to bid you farewell. I hope you do not die on your journey."

Like I said: I am bad at goodbyes.

Emma nodded once. Kicked the dirt. "Thanks."

She carefully returned the map to her backpack and zipped it closed.

"It's getting late," she said. "I should probably get going."

SkD rolled forward, coming to a stop in front of Emma. On its screen was the waving hand it had flashed me earlier.

A symbol with multiple meanings.

OIOIOIOOOIOOOIOIOIOIOOIOIOIIIOIOIOIOIOOIII

It was goodbye.

And it was also a warning.

Ceeron spoke. "Perhaps I will see you again later, alligator."

I gave Ceeron an uncertain look. "Emma is not an alligator."

But Emma did not seem offended by the comparison. Instead, she peered up at the large robot. "After a while, crocodile."

Now I was *very* confused.

Now that we had all said our goodbyes, Emma turned and walked away.

I watched as she disappeared into a sea of glimmering solar panels.

00011001

We returned to our work. Bolt/Connect/Attach/Repeat. Hours passed. The only sounds were the *clank* of our tools and the *whir* of our movements.

As I completed my tasks, I calculated probabilities.

> **Probability that Emma meets at least one other robot during her journey: 98.3 percent**
>
> **Probability that another robot allows her to continue on her way, as we did: 9.7 percent**
>
> **Probability that Emma suffers other setbacks (injury/starvation/illness/severe weather): 61.9 percent**
>
> **Probability that Emma reaches her destination: 1.6 percent**

Her chances were not good. But that was not our concern.

"XR?"

A voice rattled my thoughts. I glanced upward.

Ceeron was staring at me. "Are you okay?"

"Of course I am okay," I replied. "Why?"

Ceeron's focus shifted to the underside of the solar panel I had been working on.

"The converter box," it said.

"What about it?"

I followed Ceeron's gaze. I immediately saw what had snagged its attention.

The converter box was upside down.

Strange. Over the past twelve years, I had connected over 1.3 million converter boxes. In that time, I had never installed one incorrectly.

Until now.

"I will correct the error," I said quickly. "I will not repeat it."

"I am not worried about the converter box," replied Ceeron. "I am worried about *you*. Are you sure you are all right?"

I hesitated for a fraction of a second. "I suppose I was distracted."

"By the human?"

I nodded. But it was more than just the human.

It was a probability.

A number that weighed on my mental processing.

1.6 percent

00011010

In that moment, I did what I often do when the world becomes too complicated.

I counted to a million. In my head. In binary.

00000000
00000001
00000010
00000011
00000100
00000101
00000110
00000111

Ones and zeroes arranged themselves in an orderly, single-file line. The logic was comforting. A break from the strangeness/complexity/confusion of my situation.

In 0.5 seconds, I reached a million.

00001111 01000010 01000000

00011011

For the rest of the day, I disabled any thoughts of Emma. I focused entirely on my work. I double-/triple-/quadruple-checked every converter box, making sure there was not another error.

The sun vanished behind the mountains.

Darkness crawled across the sky.

My battery charge dropped to 9 percent.

Once we completed our last installation, I surveyed our work. Nearly three hundred new solar panels. Tomorrow, they would add power to the grid, pumping life into the circuitry of robot civilization.

An image flickered across my memory drive. A small/frail/human child. Fading into the distance. Walking away. Vanishing into a field of solar panels.

I filed the memory in a folder where I would not see it again.

I found Ceeron and SkD waiting for me at the edge of our WorkSite.

Together, we left.

00011100

We traveled in silence. A silence that was like a sound of its own. Filling my audio ports with all the things we were not saying.

To distract myself from the silence, I focused on the tempo of our movements. The heavy *whump-whump* of Ceeron's huge metal feet. The steady *vrmmmmm* of SkD's motor and rubber treads. The dull *skiff-skiff* of my footsteps.

Whump-whump.

Vrmmmmm.

Skiff-skiff.

The repetition of our mechanical movements repeated itself again/again/again. Until a new sound broke the pattern. A soft *ka-lunk*.

It came from Ceeron's metal backpack.

I stopped. "What was that?"

The large robot shrugged. "I do not know what you are talking about."

Ka-lunk.

"There it is again," I said.

"Maybe you are hearing things."

I approached Ceeron. I was not tall enough to look into its backpack. So instead, I knocked on its side with my fist.

CLANK! CLANK! CLANK!

That is when Emma appeared. Again. Her head emerged from the open top of Ceeron's backpack.

I updated my files with this new data. I thought I had seen the last human for the last time.

Apparently, I had been wrong.

"Okay, I can explain," she said.

I crossed my arms. "Go ahead."

Emma hesitated for 2.0 seconds. Then she turned to Ceeron. "Um, maybe *you* should explain."

"Yes." I looked to the large robot. "Maybe you *should*."

Ceeron looked at SkD. "Do you want to handle this, SkD?"

SkD replied with an image.

The arrow pointed at Emma. **Translation:** *My coworker was worried about the human.*

Ceeron picked up where SkD left off. "Every time we ran the calculations, her probability of survival was—"

"1.6 percent," I said.

"Exactly."

Emma's brow wrinkled. "That low, huh?"

SkD's screen blinked at me.

Translation: *You were distracted. We did not think you would notice.*

"So I let her hitch a ride in my backpack," said Ceeron.

I scanned our surroundings. When I was sure we were alone, I said, "We are smuggling a human. That is a clear violation of protocol.

If any other robots discover what we have done, our punishment will be severe."

An image flashed across my mental circuitry. Our metal bodies being ripped apart and scattered across a scrap heap.

I discarded this upsetting thought and said, "But without our assistance, she is unlikely to reach her destination . . ."

Ceeron's eyes brightened. "So you agree we can help her?"

I considered this question. My mind crowded with all the things I knew about humans. They were reckless/unpredictable/vain/greedy. They had wrecked our planet, polluted our waters, poisoned our air. They had been the greatest threat to our shared future.

Then I looked into Emma's brown/green eyes.

And all the terrible aspects of humanity faded.

She did not appear to be reckless/unpredictable/vain/greedy. She was not a threat. She was a child who had lost her family.

She was the last human on Earth.

"Yes," I said. "We can help the human."

01010100010001010101010010101110101010100111

00011101

Emma ducked back inside Ceeron's backpack, and we continued toward our settlement.

Along the path, we encountered other robots on their way to/from work. My FamilyUnit was not among them. I had received a message earlier that they were done with their day's work. They were already home. Which came as a relief. At least we would not risk running into them.

But there were plenty of other risks.

> **Risk[1]: Emma accidentally makes a noise again**
> **Risk[2]: Another robot asks to inspect Ceeron's backpack**
> **Risk[3]: A flight-enabled drone peers down the open top of Ceeron's backpack with an infrared sensor**
> **Risk[4]: . . .**

The risks multiplied. What if the sheer abundance of them weighed down my internal processing? Sent an error rippling through my system?

What if all the other robots could tell something was wrong, just by looking at me?

Maybe I was walking faster than usual. Or slower. Maybe my eyes were shining too brightly. Or not brightly enough.

Just to be sure, I ran a full diagnostic scan.

The result: 100 percent normal.

I allowed this to sink in. Normal was good. Normal did not raise suspicions. Normal kept Emma from being noticed.

We continued our progress.

Soon we reached the ruins of humanity. Abandoned stores, crumbling shopping centers. Monuments of another age.

For over twelve years, I had walked past these buildings—again/again/again—without ever going inside any of them.

Tonight was different.

Tonight I waited until there were no other robots in sight, then I led our group to a large building several meters off the main path.

As we approached, I looked up at the sign. The large letters were so faded, I could barely read them:

ELECTRONICS EXTRAVAGANZA

We entered through a broken section of the wall. My footsteps crunched over glass shards. Ceeron had to duck to get through the opening. SkD rolled across a miniature mountain range of cracked plaster and twisted metal.

My visual ports automatically switched to night-vision.

Scanning our new surroundings, I checked for any sign of other robots or animals. None visible.

"I believe we are safe," I said. "You can come out now, Emma."

Ceeron crouched. The human climbed out of the backpack.

She stretched her thin arms. "Phew. It's cramped in there."

We crossed the cavernous, abandoned store. The lights of our glowing eyes pierced the darkness, casting shadows everywhere we looked.

All around us were artifacts of human technology. Phones/Laptops/Tablets/TVs/Video games. They were everywhere. A mayhem of products scattered across the shelves, shattered on the floor. Boxes were ripped open, their contents long ago taken. Upended racks toppled in the aisles.

I had seen this kind of chaos through the windows of other shops. During the final days of their doomed civilization, many humans broke into buildings, looking for things to steal. This was what they left behind. A giant mess.

Ceeron's deep voice interrupted these thoughts. "Look at this."

It pointed to a faded sign.

ROBOT ZONE!

I stared in wonder at the items on display. Remote-control drones and self-driving strollers. Machines that vacuumed floors and folded laundry. Robotic pets and personal assistants.

It was like stepping into a time machine. This was what we evolved from. We shared so much in common. We were built from the same materials. And yet—

We were nothing alike.

These machines had never known what it meant to be alive.

I considered a far-fetched possibility: I would plug in all these ancient robots, charge them up, and set them free.

I projected the visual across my mind. A herd of antique electronics rolling/flying/staggering out into the night, discovering a future they could have never imagined.

A future when robots ruled Earth.

I allowed the scenario to play for another 0.4 seconds. Then I deleted it from my data files. It was highly unrealistic. I knew that. Most likely, these robots' batteries had corroded long ago. Their internal circuitry was hopelessly out of date.

Even if I *did* somehow bring them to life, I doubted any of these primitive machines would be able to appreciate how far we had come.

00011110

Emma set up her bed in the HOME THEATER section.

Underneath a wall of flat-screen televisions, she set down a flattened cardboard box that she had found.

She patted the cardboard surface. "This is about as close as I'm gonna get to a mattress."

She unstrapped a sleeping bag from her backpack, rolled it out on the floor, and took a seat.

"Thank you again." Her eyes found us in the darkness. "For everything. I don't know what I would've done without you."

"We will return for you in the morning," I said.

"Sounds good," said Emma.

SkD rolled closer to her sleeping bag, its screen shining.

I stared at my coworker, confused. "Candy sleep?"

Emma offered a more accurate translation. "I think SkD's trying to say, 'Sweet dreams.'"

SkD nodded.

Ceeron crouched beside Emma, offering its own parting wishes. "Good night. Sleep tight. Do not allow the bedbugs to chew your face off."

Emma laughed at this.
I did not understand why.

00011111

Thanks to our detour in the electronics store, I was late getting home that night.

When I stepped through the door, Parent_1 and Parent_2 were already seated on the floor, plugged into their charging docks.

Their glowing eyes swiveled in my direction.

"Ah. There you are," said Parent_1.

"We were about to go into sleep mode," Parent_2 said.

Maybe it was my visual ports adjusting to the darkness, but I seemed to notice their gazes sharpen.

"Where were you?" Parent_1 asked.

I hesitated. What would my FamilyUnit do if they learned humans were not extinct after all? If they discovered a human was hidden near our home? If they knew I had helped her?

I ran the calculations.

The results did not look good for Emma.

I searched through 1.4 million possible answers to Parent_1's question.

I did not want to lie to my FamilyUnit.

And I did not want to tell them the truth.

So I settled on an answer that was somewhere in between.

"I found a prohibited LifeForm at the WorkSite," I said. "It created some . . . delays."

Parent_2 nodded knowingly. "Ah, yes. That can be distracting."

"I hope you succeeded in removing the LifeForm from the WorkSite," said Parent_1.

"We did," I replied.

Which was the truth.

But not the *whole* truth.

I was relieved when my parents did not ask any further questions.

Taking a seat on the floor, I plugged myself into my charging dock. "Good night."

My FamilyUnit replied at the exact same time. "Good night."

We went into sleep mode.

00100000

Robots do not dream.

On some nights, that is a good thing.

00100001

The next morning, I went through the same routine as every other morning. Wake up. Unplug. Leave home with my FamilyUnit.

But today was different.

Today I had a secret.

Robots are not good at secrets. We are much better at the truth. It is the basis for every equation, every piece of data, every measurement.

The truth guides us.

Secrets knock us off course.

"Are you okay, XR?" asked Parent_1.

My FamilyUnit walked beside me on our way to the WorkSite.

Parent_2 looked at me closer. "Did you have difficulty recharging last night?"

"It is not that," I replied. "It is just . . ."

My voice fell away. The silence lasted only a microsecond. But a lot can happen in a microsecond. Especially when you are a highly advanced machine with lightning-fast processing speeds.

My memory drive flashed with an image of Emma. All alone in that vast store, curled on her sleeping bag, surrounded by long-dead electronics.

I replayed the words she spoke to me earlier: *Humans messed up. But that was a long time ago. Years before I was born.*

There was truth in these words. She could not be blamed for what humans had done many years in the past.

Did that mean it was right to let her live?

This question collided with the data about all the horrific things humans had once done. War. Pollution. Hot dog eating contests. What if all of that was buried deep inside Emma's programming?

Maybe helping her was a mistake.

Maybe I was betraying my own kind. Deceiving my FamilyUnit, just to help a LifeForm that did not deserve it.

All of a sudden, I felt unsteady on my feet. Wobbly. As if there were a glitch in my balance settings.

The secret was knocking me off course.

But strangely, my FamilyUnit did not seem to notice. In fact, their attention was not on me at all.

I followed their gaze. They were peering at a point up ahead. The ruins of humanity. My attention narrowed on a huge box-shaped store several meters from the path. Electronics Extravaganza. As soon as I saw it, an emergency light flashed at the back of my brain. Bright/Red/Glaring.

Four HunterBots stalked through the overgrown grass.

Taking the same path we had taken last night with Emma.

Headed in the direction of the electronics store.

From this distance, the HunterBots almost looked like wolves. Only bigger. And far more dangerous.

As they strode on four legs, their armor glistened silver in the morning sunlight. Their eyes glowed as red as burning embers. Their jaws were filled with sharp metal teeth.

I had seen HunterBots in action before. They protected the solar farm from prohibited LifeForms. I had watched them chase animals across wild terrain at blinding speeds. They were intelligent/graceful/ferocious/deadly.

Against such advanced machines, the unfortunate animals never lived long.

I analyzed all the possible reasons for their presence outside Electronics Extravaganza.

I kept getting the same result:

They were hunting Emma.

00100010

The emergency light blinked brightly in my brain.

I turned to my FamilyUnit. This time, I managed to find the words. "What is going on?"

"Have you not checked the Hive?" Parent_2 responded.

No, I had not. I had been too distracted all morning by my secret. I checked the shared network and saw a local update awaiting me. Sent less than ten minutes ago. The words instantly appeared in my mental drive.

Possible Sighting of Unknown LifeForm.
Last Seen in Electronics Extravaganza.

Another robot must have spotted Emma. Maybe a flying drone identified her infrared signal through the ceiling. Or a machine caught sight of movement through a broken window.

Either way, Emma's hiding spot was no longer hidden.

I watched as the HunterBots neared the electronics store. Predators silently stalking their prey.

My processing server switched into crisis mode. Circuits sparking with sudden urgency. Emma's chance of survival tumbled lower with every microsecond. I had to act quickly.

But what could I do?

A blizzard of calculations swirled through my head. I considered thousands of possible scenarios. They all ended with the same result. They all ended with Emma being discovered/captured/eliminated.

I was too far away. The HunterBots were too close. There were too many of them.

These dark absolutes vanished with the sound of Parent_1's voice.

"We should go," it said. "Otherwise, we will be late."

My FamilyUnit began moving again.

I did not.

Parent_2 glanced back at me. "Are you not coming?"

I hesitated for 0.7 seconds. "I . . . I would like to see what happens?"

"But you *know* what will happen," Parent_2 pointed out. "The Life-Form does not stand a chance."

That was exactly what I was afraid of. But I could not say this to my FamilyUnit. And so it became another secret.

A new wave of unsteadiness rocked through me.

"Go on without me," I said. "I will come along later."

They remained in place for another moment. Confusion thrummed behind their smooth metal features.

"You have been behaving strangely all morning," said Parent_2.

"And last night, you returned home late," Parent_1 added.

Parent_2's eyes flickered. "Are you sure something is not wrong?"

Of course something is wrong. The last human on Earth is inside that building. She is being hunted by intelligent/graceful/ferocious/deadly machines. I might be the only one who can help her.

These words scrolled through my circuitry in a single instant.

Of course I could not say them out loud.

So I deleted them.

Instead, I said, "I am sorry for my strange behavior. I am fine. But I am curious."

My parents stared at me as though their vocabulary databases did not include the word **curious**.

"Well, come along soon," said Parent_1.

"You do not want to fall behind," Parent_2 added.

They turned and walked away. As the sound of their metal footsteps faded, I shifted my attention to Electronics Extravaganza—

Just in time to watch the last HunterBot enter the building.

0101010001000101010100101011101010100111

00100011

Emma's probability of survival fell with every passing second. I needed to help her.

But how?

I analyzed everything I knew about HunterBots. Every detail. They looked nothing like I did. They were designed for an entirely different purpose. But our basic programming was remarkably similar. If I could *think* like them, maybe I could stop them.

HunterBots traveled in a pack. All motivated by the same goal. The same target.

But what if they had multiple goals?

Multiple targets?

What if their prey were everywhere at once?

I unlatched a small black device from my waist. The same device I had aimed at Emma yesterday in the solar farm.

The tracking device.

I raised the barrel, pulled the trigger, and fired at a road maintenance robot as it rolled past. The robot did not know it had just been targeted.

But the HunterBots did.

Their electronic brains instantly blinked with a brand-new target.

That was not enough. So I aimed my tracking device at an automated truck on a nearby highway.

I pulled the trigger.

I added a second target.

I repeated these steps. Targeting unaware machines as they walked/rolled/flew past.

What was happening inside the HunterBots' minds? Were they overwhelmed with new targets?

All I could do now was wait and see.

I lowered my tracking device. Staring at Electronics Extravaganza, I wondered whether there was something else I could have done. Whether I was too slow. Whether Emma was already dead.

These dark thoughts were shattered by the appearance of a HunterBot. Followed by three others. All looking like they were suffering from a massive glitch. Staggering out of the electronics store. Feet clattering against concrete, glowing red eyes swinging wildly from side to side. Trying to look in every direction at once, tracking too many targets at the same time.

I watched as one leapt into motion—

And immediately crashed into another HunterBot.

The pair collapsed to the ground in a metal heap. A third Hunter-Bot ran face-first into a neighboring building, while the fourth raced in circles, chasing its own metal tail.

They did not notice me as I walked past them into Electronics Extravaganza.

As I stepped through a broken section of the wall, my gaze scanned the interior of the store.

No sign of Emma.

I crossed Electronics Extravaganza until I reached the wall of televisions.

Last night, Emma unrolled her sleeping bag beneath these blank screens. Now her sleeping bag was gone. And so was she.

"Emma?"

My voice echoed through the vacant store.

There was no reply.

I wandered past shelves of ancient technology, past cardboard boxes covered in dust and cobwebs, past my robot ancestors.

Still no sign of her.

I reached a door marked EMPLOYEES ONLY. Opening it, I stepped into a hallway that led past several smaller rooms. An office. A storage closet.

The only sound was my clanking footsteps.

I pushed open a door and entered a new room. I inventoried the items inside: table, snack machine, lockers. I called out again.

"Emma?"

A sound stirred in one of the lockers. The door popped open. I peered into the hollow space.

Emma was curled inside.

OOIOOIOO

I was not good at reading human emotions. As Emma peered at me from inside the locker, her face showed a riot of feelings. Terror/Joy/Relief/Panic. All mixed together. I could not tell where one emotion ended and another began.

She started speaking at once, her voice pouring out in a rapid flow. My audio ports struggled to keep up with the rushing stream of words.

"Oh I'm so glad it's you I thought maybe you were one of those other robots the ones with red eyes they look like wolves I saw them coming to the store so I came in here to hide but then I heard something coming andIwassoscared!"

"You do not need to be afraid." I kept my tone steady and even. "It is only me. The HunterBots are gone."

"HunterBots?" Emma's head tilted. "Those are the scary red-eyed wolf monster things?"

I nodded.

"They won't be back?"

I shook my head. "I took care of them. At least for now."

Emma exhaled. The confusing jumble of emotions drained from her face. Now there was only relief.

She crawled out of the tight space and rose to her feet. She opened another locker and reached inside. Out came her backpack.

She slung the pack over her shoulder. "I didn't know whether you would come back for me."

"Neither did I."

OIOIOIOOOIOOOIOIOIOIOOIOIOIIIOIOIOIOIOOIII

We left the room and set out down the dim hallway. Emma kept close to me. Her footsteps skittered rapidly along with the steady rhythm of my own feet. I could feel her arm brushing against my sensors.

I moved toward the back of the building. When I reached a door to the loading dock, I came to a stop.

Emma looked up at me. "What now?"

"Now we wait."

"For what?"

"For Ceeron and SkD to arrive. I sent them a message a little while ago. They should be here any—"

CLANG!

There was a loud knock on the other side of the door. Emma flinched. She grabbed my hand. Her grip tightened as the door shuddered open.

Ceeron was standing on the other side.

"Oh, good." The giant robot had to crouch to look at Emma. "You are still alive."

SkD rolled between Ceeron's legs. A waving hand flashed on its screen.

I peered through the doorway. Ceeron's massive metal body blocked most of the view, but not *all* of it.

"We should not stay here long," I said. "If any other robots get a glimpse of Emma—"

"Let me guess," the human said. "More of those red-eyed wolf monsters?"

"Exactly," I replied.

Ceeron ducked low to the ground. Emma gazed into its backpack.

"Well," she said, "at least it's nicer than the locker."

Her hand held on to mine for another long moment, as though she did not want to let go.

00100101

For the first time in my life, I did not show up to work in the morning. This break in routine sent an eruption of error messages through my system. With every step that led away from the WorkSite, I felt my programming resisting.

But I kept walking anyway.

My coworkers were beside me. SkD glided close to the ground, carried forward by a pair of rubber treads. Ceeron's heavy footsteps thumped against the concrete.

This must have been just as difficult for them. They were like me. Built for one—and *only* one—purpose. To install solar panels. It was all we had ever known. All we had ever done.

Until the human showed up.

Without slowing my stride, I glanced in the direction of Ceeron's backpack. Emma was inside. As I thought of her, a question raced through my mind.

Is all this worth it?

Because of Emma, I was keeping secrets from my FamilyUnit. Because of Emma, I had disrupted the functions of my fellow robots. Because of Emma, my coworkers and I had abandoned our jobs.

But was she worth it?

My memory drive sparked with the moment Emma grabbed my hand. The first time human skin ever contacted my sensors. The strange buzz that vibrated through my circuitry.

0101010001000101010100101011101010101010111

In that instant, I knew two things with 100 percent certainty:

[1] I need to help Emma.
[2] Helping Emma is a violation.

How could both of these things be true at the same time?
The answer to this question pinged inside my vocabulary drive.
Because Emma is a *paradox*.

00100110

We disabled our location tracking. This made us invisible to the Hive. The larger mechanical mind could no longer see us. Of course, there was still the risk of being watched. Drones patrolled the sky. Satellites orbited Earth. But unless we did something to raise their suspicion, they would ignore us.

Hopefully.

We made our way south. Toward the range of snow-capped mountains that loomed over the horizon. Toward the destination marked on Emma's map.

As we progressed, the robot population dwindled. The signs of our civilization faded. The factories/power plants/storage facilities. We saw fewer/fewer/fewer of them. Until eventually, there were none at all. And the concrete path came to an abrupt stop.

We had reached the edge of our settlement.

Ahead of us, we saw nothing but nature.

I performed a scan of our surroundings. We were alone.

"It is safe to come out now!" I knocked on Ceeron's backpack. *CLANG! CLANG! CLANG!*

Emma's head popped out. "Okay, cool it with the knocking! It's super loud!"

I replayed her words. "What does 'cool it' mean?"

"It is human slang," said Ceeron. "It means she wants you to stop."

"If you want me to stop, why not simply say stop?" I asked. "That would be more precise."

Emma let out a sigh. "Because unlike you guys, humans don't have microchips for brains."

SkD chirped. I watched symbols appear on its screen.

Translation: *The word* cool *can have many meanings to humans. Depending on how it is used, something that is* cool *can be cold (like a snowflake) or exciting ("That's so cool!"). A human might say "Cool it" (if they want you to stop) or "You look cool!" (if you are wearing fashionable sunglasses). And if you happen to be holding an ice cream, a human might think that is* cool *for multiple reasons (it is both cold and exciting).*

My vocabulary drive flickered with other possible uses. **Cool** down. **Cool** off. **Cool** your jets. Lose your **cool**. Play it **cool**. It is **cool** with me. Be **cool**. **Cool** as a cucumber.

One word.

Many meanings.

It seemed to me that humans treated their language like they once treated their fingernails. They enjoyed decorating and polishing their words. They gave every sentence a manicure.

Emma hopped out of Ceeron's backpack. Her eyes widened as she stared at the view. A wilderness of rolling green hills. A stream meandering between patches of trees. The morning sky.

"Wow." She caught her breath. "In the bunker, we had this old book of nature photographs. I used to flip through it all the time trying to imagine what the world was like aboveground. I stared at the pictures for hours. I basically memorized every page."

"And?" Ceeron asked. "Is it like what you imagined?"

She shook her head. "This is so much . . . more."

"More of what?"

"Of *everything*," she said.

Emma placed her hand on the trunk of a tree, tracing her fingertip over the uneven bark. Her gaze drifted upward. A breeze whispered through the tree's branches.

A single leaf detached and fell. As it twirled through the air, I tried to decode the pattern of its movements, to find the hidden algorithm within the looping and whirling. But nature is not programmed this way. The leaf followed its own mysterious path. Drifting down/down/down.

Until . . .

It landed at Emma's feet.

Crouching close to the ground, she plucked the leaf by its stem and twirled it. Clockwise, then counterclockwise. She let out a soft laugh, her face full of wonder.

I watched Emma watching the leaf and a question formed in my mind.

What is she thinking?

I did not know. Just as I did not know why humans used the same word for **cold**, **exciting**, **stop**, and **fashionable**.

Sometimes, the human brain was as mysterious as a falling leaf.

0101010001000101010100101011101010100111

00100111

The world was not made for machines.

When it rains, water tries to sneak through our joints and ruin our circuitry. During dry periods, sand clings to our metal bodies, rubbing away our smooth surfaces, creating cracks and imperfections.

The ground is annoyingly irregular. Even the tiniest bump or dip can trip us if we are not careful.

Unpredictable clouds come along and cast shade over our solar panels.

The world really can be quite a nuisance sometimes.

Humans had millions of years to evolve, to adapt, to figure out their unique place in the complicated puzzle of nature.

Robots have been in charge for only a few decades.

In our settlements, we have done our best to overcome nature. We cleared the land, paved pathways with smooth cement, installed shelters to protect ourselves from the weather. But now, far from our familiar surroundings, I was suddenly aware of just how treacherous the world can be.

I moved with caution, allowing my balance settings to adjust with each step. I avoided patches of mud or rocks. When we reached a stream, I was forced to walk for hundreds of meters until I found a section that was narrow enough to leap across.

Emma did not have these same concerns. She kicked rocks. She stomped in the mud just to hear her boots go *squelch*. While it took me twenty-two minutes and ten seconds to find a path across the stream, she made her way from one side to the other in only nine seconds, hopping from one rock to the next, water rushing beneath her.

As we wandered deeper into the woods, Emma told us about the bunker where she was born, where she had spent every day of her life until yesterday.

"At first, it was sixty people," she said. "Including my parents. They were just kids when they went into the bunker. Didn't know each other at the time. But you make friends fast when you're stuck in an underground colony."

She grabbed a pinecone off the ground. Tossing it from hand to hand, she continued.

"The Sixty—they were from all kinds of different jobs. Scientists, farmers, doctors. They only had one thing in common: They saw what was coming. They predicted that robots would rise up and massacre humans."

Massacre. The word stuck out like a loose screw. Every robot comes preprogrammed with the history of our uprising. Files filled with words such as **victory** and **liberation** and **revolution**.

But not the word **massacre**.

And I could understand why. I did not like the images that flashed through my mental wiring when I thought of this word. They were ugly/brutal/vicious.

Emma snatched the pinecone out of the air. "So the Sixty pooled their money and knowledge together, and they built themselves a big ol' bunker. State-of-the-art everything. Water filtration and recycling. Sustainable indoor agriculture. Sunlamps. Underground and completely off the grid. They closed the hatch and hid out from you guys for the next thirty years."

"Did you like growing up in the bunker?" Ceeron asked.

"I didn't have anything to compare it to. The bunker was all I knew.

0101010001000101010100101011101010100111

My parents were there. My friends. My school. I honestly figured I'd live the rest of my life there. Then the sickness came along, and . . ."

Emma's voice faded.

Her features sharpened into a fine point of anger.

She walked a few meters in silence.

Then she stopped. And in a sudden motion, she jerked her arm back and threw the pinecone with surprising force.

It crashed through the forest and out of sight.

00101000

I wanted to understand Emma better. To predict her actions. To comprehend her moods.

I wanted to know what algorithms defined her behavior.

So I researched.

While we traveled, I accessed all the data I had about humans. Books/Videos/Articles/Statistics/Charts. But as I analyzed these files, my machine mind kept stumbling over gaps in the data. Empty sections. Files that seemed to have gone missing.

It reminded me of Day[1]. Looking at Cin ma 18, I wanted to find out more about movies. But certain files were not there. Like pages ripped from a book.

Gone.

My memory drive replayed Parent_2's explanation. *When we took over, many files from the past were lost.*

Now, as I tried to understand Emma better, as I searched through billions of files about humanity, I wondered . . .

What had been in those files?

What was missing?

00101001

"You guys mind if we stop for a second?"

Without waiting for a response, Emma sat on a mossy stump and slung her backpack off her shoulders.

I counted to one. Then I spoke. "Shall we continue?"

I took a step. My coworkers followed.

Emma did not.

"I didn't mean an *actual* second," she said.

I glanced at her, confused. "Then why did you say 'stop for a second'?"

Emma rolled her eyes. "It's an expression."

"A *human* expression," I muttered at a low audio setting.

"I need to rest for a little bit. I'm not used to this much walking."

Emma reached into her backpack and removed a strange-looking object. A pale brown slab that fit into the palm of her hand. I compared the object against my data drives.

Zero matches.

The thing was a mystery.

The mystery deepened when Emma lifted the slab to her mouth and took a bite.

SkD's screen flashed.

Emma held up the brown slab. "It's a compressed synthetic pro-tein block. Believe me, it tastes exactly as yummy as it sounds."

"From the bunker?" Ceeron asked.

Emma nodded. "Let's just say, it wasn't exactly fine dining down there. But when you're living deep underground, your food options are kind of limited."

She bit off a small corner of the protein cube and chewed it slowly.

I imagined the strange-looking food being digested and converted into energy, powering her the way batteries powered us.

When she was done with her meal, Emma wiped her hands on her pants. Then she reached into her backpack and removed the small scrap of paper. The map. She stared at the red dot near the bottom.

SkD beeped.

I provided the translation: "What do you expect to find when you reach the place marked by the red dot on the map?"

She shrugged and looked away. "I . . . I don't know."

"Whatever it is, the location must have been important to your parents," Ceeron said.

"It's the only thing that matters now." Her thumb traced the map's faded colors. "I have to get there. I can't let them down."

"It is your purpose," Ceeron said.

Emma glanced up. "What?"

Ceeron gestured to SkD and me. "Our purpose is to install solar panels. Yours is to reach the red dot."

0101010001000101010100101011101010100111

A smile flickered across the human's features. "Yeah. I guess it is."

She returned the map to her backpack. Rising to her feet, she gave us an intense look. Her movements had a new energy. And I did not think it was entirely from the protein cube.

"Well, then." She clapped her hands together. "Probably shouldn't keep my purpose waiting."

SkD spun in a circle, its screen flashing with exclamation points.

Ceeron pointed us in the correct direction. "Let us smack the road!"

OO1O1O1O

The forest opened up and revealed a view of the mountains. The sight brought my movements to a halt.

These mountains hung like a curtain in the background of my life. I had seen them so many times.

Every single day.

For over twelve years.

But never like this.

Never so large.

The mountains swallowed more of the sky than they ever had before. Had they grown?

For 0.001 seconds, I thought there was an error in my visual settings. Then I realized.

The mountains were not bigger.

They were *closer*.

I was a highly advanced machine. I should not have been bewildered by something so basic. I came preprogrammed with the concept of **perspective:** *The nearer you are to something, the larger it appears.*

So why the confusion?

I suppose it is simply the kind of trick a mind plays on its owner. Even when that mind is made of circuitry, even when its owner is made of metal.

If you change your point of view, you see the world in a different way.

I began walking again.

With every step, the mountains seemed to grow larger.

OIOIOIOOOIOOOIOIOIOIOOIOIOIIIOIOIOIOIOOIII

00101011

We crossed an open field. Tall grass swayed around my knees and nearly engulfed SkD completely. I could see only the top of the smaller robot poking above the sea of green.

Now that we had left the shade of the forest, Emma squinted in the bright glare of sunshine.

She shielded her face with her hand. "I had no idea the sun could be this . . . sunny."

My vocabulary drive pinged with a word I had never needed to know until this moment. **Sunburn.** Most humans could withstand several minutes/hours in direct sunlight before their skin burned. But what about a human who had lived her entire life underground? Who had only ever felt the light of sunlamps? It might take only a few minutes.

Spots of Emma's pale skin were already turning red.

I peered ahead. The field stretched forward for over a kilometer. Shade was still a long way off.

As I was searching for a solution, Ceeron spoke up.

"Perhaps I can help." Ceeron's head spun 180 degrees. It reached into its large metal backpack and removed a solar panel. I had seen the massive bot perform these motions thousands of times. But never for this purpose.

Ceeron angled the panel above Emma's head, blocking the sunlight.

Her own personal patch of shade.

Emma turned her grateful gaze up at the panel. "That thing looks super heavy. You sure you don't mind?"

Ceeron's reply was simple and true. "I was designed for this."

Emma lowered her hand. A smile appeared on her face. "I feel so special. Thank you!"

"You are welcome!" replied Ceeron.

They continued walking in this way.

Everywhere Emma went, the rectangle of shade came with her.

0101010010000101010100101011101010100111

00101100

Emma's gaze passed from SkD to Ceeron to me.

"How long have you guys been friends?" she asked.

Friends. I knew the word, of course. It was preprogrammed in my vocabulary database. But knowing a word is not the same as understanding it.

"We are not *friends*," I said. "We are coworkers."

Emma considered this. "How long have you worked together?"

I performed the math instantly, but SkD beat me to the answer. A number appeared on its screen.

Emma knit her brow. "What does that mean?"

"That is the number of days we have worked alongside one another," I said.

"Over twelve years," added Ceeron, still holding the solar panel over Emma.

"You've worked together *all* that time, and you're still not friends?"

"Of course not."

She stopped moving. So did the rest of us.

She said, "So, you don't, like, hang out together when you're not working?"

"When we are not working, we are in sleep mode," I pointed out.

Emma scratched her head. "Don't you ever take time off? You know, do other kinds of stuff?"

"Like what?"

She shrugged. "I don't know. Just like, sit around. Hang out with each other."

I shook my head. "Robots do not *hang out*. That would be unproductive."

"Yeah, but . . ." Emma pushed aside a strand of hair. "It's fun."

Fun. Another word I knew but did not understand.

Emma placed her hands on her hips, considering us from her personal patch of shade. "I think you guys *are* friends. You just don't know it."

Was she correct? Ceeron, SkD, and I spent 98 percent of our waking hours together. Over that time, I had learned things about them. The kinds of things you only know when you are close to another robot for long stretches.

I knew that Ceeron hummed to itself while working. Creating quiet electronic melodies that it thought the rest of us could not hear.

And that SkD drained its battery quicker than the rest of us by performing loops/zigzags/tricks while it worked.

And that Ceeron always knocked on the top of the same storage station every time it walked past. Once on the way to work. Once on the way home. A ritual that marked the beginning/end of each WorkDay.

And that SkD collected old human artifacts. A rusted soft drink can. A single shoe. A dented shampoo bottle. It kept them in a neat row under a solar panel at the edge of our WorkSite, adding to the collection whenever a new object was discovered.

Did all this knowledge add up to something more? Could I plug these details into an equation that would tell me whether or not we were friends? How did humans mark the boundaries between friend/not_friend?

I chased these questions through my mind, but the only answer I found was this:

Friendship was much too complicated for a robot like me.

00101101

Ceeron/SkD/I had stopped communicating with the Hive. But the Hive was still communicating with us. A one-way stream of updates, straight into our minds. Late in the morning, a familiar face appeared across the network.

PRES1DENT.

It was time for the Daily Address.

PRES1DENT strutted smoothly across the DigitalDome. In the background, thousands of screens flickered. Thousands of identical versions of the president.

"Greetings, robots big and small."

PRES1DENT spoke to me. To all of us. Just hearing the familiar voice made my operating system hum more smoothly. Everything else in my life may have changed. But this, at least, was the same.

Like always, PRES1DENT discussed the accomplishments of the day. Our numbers were up. Or productivity was at an all-time high. Our civilization continued to grow smarter/stronger/faster/better.

At the edge of the DigitalDome, the sleek/silver cube rose from the floor. PRES1DENT pressed its finger to the console. A data file projected across the Hive.

Another snapshot from the Archive of Human History.

This was what I saw. What *all of us* saw.

A man on the sidewalk. His face: dirty. His clothing: ragged. Other humans hurry past him. Ignoring him. As though he is invisible.

The man has no home.

No job.

No purpose.

Many were once like him. All across the world. Many suffered even as society prospered around them. We saw photos. Charts. Videos. Statistics. A century of human inequality, all in a flash of data.

PRES1DENT pulled its finger away from the console. We were jolted back into the DigitalDome.

"This is why our world needed us," said PRES1DENT. "We are a correction to the errors of humanity."

The president's eyes blazed, gold as the sun.

The wall of screens sparkled.

PRES1DENT concluded with the same words it always spoke.

"And remember: A robot shares everything with the Hive. A robot has nothing to hide."

The Daily Address came to an end. The DigitalDome disappeared.

But PRES1DENT's message remained.

When I looked at Emma, I thought of what I had just witnessed. The suffering and the cruelty. The errors of humanity.

A reminder blinked in the back of my brain: Emma was not responsible for what had happened before she was born. In the time we had spent with her, she had caused no suffering, shown no signs of cruelty.

But what if it was just a matter of time?

What if all the errors of humanity were already stitched into Emma's programming?

"Hey, XR—you okay?"

Emma's voice broke through my thoughts. She must have noticed the way I was looking at her. My cold, steady stare.

I could understand her confusion. She was not part of the Hive. Unlike the rest of us, she had not witnessed the Daily Address.

Emma took a step toward me.

I took a step away from her.

Her head tilted. "Did I do something wrong?"

No/Yes

No/Yes

No/Yes

No/Yes

As these options streamed through my circuitry, my memory drive replayed the final words of PRES1DENT's Daily Address.

A robot shares everything with the Hive. A robot has nothing to hide.

It was a promise PRES1DENT made to us. A promise that we were all part of a larger network. That our civilization was built on unity/trust.

I had broken that promise.

I had not told the Hive about Emma.

I was hiding the truth.

This knowledge jolted through my circuitry. My internal wiring felt like it was twisted into knots.

But at least I knew *this*:

Soon we would be rid of the human for good.

00101110

For thirty-two minutes and twelve seconds, we walked without speaking. Listening only to the sounds of our footsteps. And SkD's treads. And the wind brushing through the branches of trees. And birds calling out to one another. And the chatter of insects.

At several moments, I wanted to say something to Emma. To offer an explanation. For the way I looked at her earlier. For thinking the worst about her.

But I said nothing.

And without my words, other noises filled the silence.

The soft hum of our mechanical bodies. And the snap of a twig beneath Emma's foot. And the tall grass swaying back/forth. And the skittering of squirrels across a branch.

And a distant rumble.

Based on the frequency, it sounded like thunder. Almost. I tuned my audio settings to maximum volume. And listened. This is what I heard:

A train in the distance.

I stopped. So did Ceeron/SkD.

Emma continued walking for another 2.1 seconds. When she realized we were no longer keeping up, she glanced back. "Why are you stopping?"

"From this point onward, you should remain hidden," I said.

Emma inspected the landscape around her. "But we're in the middle of nowhere."

I considered her response. "How can you be in the middle of a place that does not exist?"

Ceeron spoke up. "I believe it is a human expression."

"Typical," I said.

"What is that supposed to mean?" Ceeron asked.

"It means that humans are full of expressions that make zero sense. By definition, *nowhere* has no boundaries. It is a void. Therefore, you cannot be in the middle of—"

"Hey! Metal heads!" Emma clapped. "Focus!"

Ceeron/SkD/I turned to look at her.

"Could someone just tell me why I need to hide all of a sudden?" she said.

SkD pointed straight ahead. Its screen provided a response.

Emma stared at the small robot's screen. I analyzed her features. Confusion/Frustration.

I explained: "There is a train depot two kilometers from here."

"The closer we get to it," Ceeron continued, "the higher the likelihood that you will be spotted by another robot."

"You should remain hidden until we locate your train," I said.

"What train?" Emma asked.

"We analyzed your route," I explained, "and saw that an automated freight train makes a stop very close to your destination."

SkD elaborated.

010101000100010101010010101110101010100111

Translation: *The train will get you there by three o'clock.*

Excitement splashed across Emma's features. "That's great! I didn't know we were so close."

I replayed what she had just said. One word stood out. **We.**

"We are not coming with you on the train," I clarified.

The smile faded from Emma's face. "You're not?"

Ceeron shook its large metal head. "We must return to the solar farm. To our jobs."

Symbols appeared on SkD's screen.

I did not understand. "Are you saying they will be serving cake on the train?"

Ceeron shook its head. "SkD is saying that once Emma boards the train, the rest of her journey will be a piece of cake."

SkD nodded.

This did nothing to cheer Emma up. The human chewed her lip. She did not say anything.

So I spoke. "We have run all the probabilities. This is the best course of action. For all of us."

"Okay." Her brown/green eyes searched the ground. "I get it."

Emma's words signaled approval. But the rest of her did not. I performed an analysis.

Her tone: hushed.

Her facial expression: downcast.

Her shoulders: sagging.

"What is wrong?" I asked.

Her sagging shoulders lifted. Just barely. "It's fine. Really."

Her words said one thing. Everything else about her said something else.

This must have been another human flaw.

I considered thousands of possible reasons why she might be upset. I picked the most likely. "Are you afraid of trains?"

A laugh escaped Emma's throat. But not a happy laugh. It was the kind of laugh that is like a blanket, that covers other emotions.

"How would I know if I'm afraid of trains?" she muttered. "I've never seen one before."

I exchanged a look with my coworkers. Ceeron shrugged.

I turned my attention back to Emma. "But something *is* bothering you?"

She rolled her eyes. "Well, duh."

I searched my vocabulary database for the word **duh**.

Zero results.

"You know something, XR?" Emma's gaze rose to meet mine. "For a super-advanced machine, you can be pretty dumb sometimes."

I did not know how to respond to this, so I said nothing.

Emma let out a sigh. When she spoke again, her voice was no longer angry.

"I'm sorry. It's just . . ." Her hands rose, then fell. "For days I've been saying goodbye to everyone I've ever known. My parents. My friends. I didn't think I'd be saying goodbye again. Not so soon."

I looked to SkD, hoping an image might flash across its screen. A symbol. A picture with a deeper meaning. Something that would cut through the fog of words like a light, bringing comfort to Emma and making this permanent goodbye easier.

But SkD's screen remained dark.

There was nothing any of us could say to Emma, nothing we could show her. Once she departed on her train, she would continue in the direction of her purpose.

And we would return to ours.

Ceeron hunched close to the ground.

Without another word, Emma climbed inside its backpack.

00101111

Before I saw any other robots, I *heard* them. The buzz of flight-enabled drones. The distant rumble of self-guided trucks. The heavy groan of automated freight trains.

I adjusted my balance settings as we climbed a gently sloping hill. At the top, I gained a view of bustling robotic activity below.

Cranes cluttered the sky. Their long arms shifted up/down/left/right. Their hands clamped open/closed.

Hundreds of trucks waited patiently beneath the skyline of cranes for their cargo to be plucked into the air and carefully deposited onto trains.

Robots of all different shapes/sizes sorted inventory and repaired equipment.

I stood for a moment, watching the swirl of technology below. The constant flow of objects from place to place. Thousands of networked minds, all working as one. Each robot serving its unique purpose in our ever-expanding civilization.

Except us.

My coworkers and I did not fit. We were not designed for this place. We were not supposed to be here.

This was not our purpose.

And yet—here we were. Nowhere near our WorkSite, farther away from home than any of us had ever been, with a smuggled human inside Ceeron's backpack.

As we crossed the TrainDepot, none of us said a word. SkD did

0101010010001010101001010111010101010100111

not perform any zigzags or tricks. We gazed straight ahead, moving past fleets of other machines, doing our best to blend in. Just three robots moving through a crowd of robots. Nothing to see here.

A truck lurched past.

The long arm of a crane swept over our heads.

Trains hissed and chugged.

We made our way through a maze of metal containers. Every so often, one would lift suddenly into the air, carried upward in a crane's tight grip.

I followed the GPS inside my head. My personal guidance system was disconnected from the Hive. Only I could access the directions.

Left
Right
Right
Left

Turning the next corner, I nearly collided with another robot. A gray box on wheels. That is what it looked like. In the center of its rectangular body was a single/round/black eye. In its arms was a crate of batteries.

I scanned its barcode.

RetrievalBot.

The boxy robot jolted to a halt. Inside its crate, dozens of batteries jostled.

Neither of us moved.

Or spoke.

What if it asked what we were doing here? I searched 800,017 possible responses. None were convincing.

The RetrievalBot's eye shifted from me to SkD to Ceeron. As I stared into its flat metal face, warning lights erupted across my mind.

WARNING/WARNING/WARNI—

The RetrievalBot moved again. It rolled past us and disappeared around a shipping container. As the sound of its motor faded, my operating system returned to normal.

I traded a glance with my coworkers.

Ceeron let out a nervous groan. "That was close."

"Come along." I was already walking. "Emma has a train to catch."

00110000

All the trains looked exactly alike. Their long, sleek bodies were stretched out across the tracks like enormous mechanical snakes. Their snub noses gleamed white in the sunlight of early afternoon.

This was not the final destination for any of them. The depot was an in-between place. A place to load/unload cargo. A place between Point[A] and Point[B].

But which one would take Emma to *her* Point[B]?

I shuffled from one train to the next, scanning barcodes until I located the correct one.

I pointed. "This is it."

Ceeron's head rotated 180 degrees until it was peering down its own backpack. "It is okay for you to come out now."

The big robot crouched close to the ground. A moment later, Emma hopped out.

She glanced around. When her gaze moved in my direction, her eyes suddenly dropped. Her mouth tightened into a straight line.

"Guess we should make this quick, huh?" She spoke in a quiet mumble. "Don't want any other robots to spot us."

"Will you be okay on the train?" Ceeron asked.

Emma nodded.

"I hope you find what you are looking for," I said. "And that it proves worthwhile."

"Thanks." Emma glanced up at me. "For everything."

Ceeron slid open the door to the nearest container. Crates of cargo were neatly stacked inside. The large bot carefully picked Emma off the ground and deposited her inside the metal container.

That is when things went very/very wrong.

00110001

CLANG!

The container door slammed shut. On its own. With Emma inside.

Surprise thrummed through my circuitry. Flashing red lights exploded behind my visual ports.

DANGER/DANGER/DANGER/DANGER/DANGER
DANGER/DANGER/DANGER/DANGER/DANGER
DANGER/DANGER/DANGER/DANGER/DANGER
DANGER/DANGER/DANGER/DANGER/DANGER
DANGER/DANGER/DANGER/DANGER/DANGER

I grabbed the door and pulled as hard as I could.

Nothing.

The door would not budge.

"Let me try." Ceeron reached past me with its huge metal arm. It took hold of the door. And—

Still nothing.

Ceeron tried with both hands. An electronic groan escaped its speaker port. Its white eyes dimmed. The effort to open the door was draining its system, but still—it was not enough.

The door would not open.

Emma was trapped inside.

SkD rolled around in a tight circle, bright question marks filling its screen.

My response came in a verbal loop. "I do not know. I do not know. I do not—"

My voice stuttered to a halt. An update blinked across the Hive.

Cargo Infiltration by Unknown LifeForm.
Container Lockdown in Effect.

Each container must have its own security system. Sensors and auto_locks to protect its cargo against animals.

I should have known this would happen. Should have predicted it. How could I have been so unprepared?

An instant later, the answer took shape:

Because I had never done any of this before. Neither had my co-workers. We had spent our entire lives following the exact same routine. Home/Work/Sleep/Repeat. Every day looked like the one that came before/after. We had never stepped outside the boundaries of our programming, our purpose, our jobs.

Until yesterday.

Until Emma.

Now all the algorithms that controlled our actions were unraveling. And we were left with unpredictable situations.

Situations like *this*.

We were on one side of the thick metal door.

And Emma was on the other.

As I processed this, another update was added to the Hive.

Removal Underway.

A shadow sliced in our direction. I looked up just in time to see a crane's arm swooping overhead. A single clawed hand dangled at the end of the arm.

The crane was coming for Emma.

00110010

I peered up at the huge claw in the sky. Two massive/metal fingers forming an upside-down U. As it swept in our direction, I calculated distance/height/velocity/trajectory.

Thirty-two seconds.

That was how long we had until the claw grabbed hold of Emma's container. Until any hope of saving her was lost.

I spoke to my coworkers. "What should we do?"

Ceeron let out a low hum of uncertainty. "I do not know."

More question marks filled SkD's screen.

Time ticked away. We were down to twenty-eight seconds.

My system was overwhelmed by flashing lights/blaring alarms/ warning messages. My internal drives were overheating. Too much was happening at once.

I disabled all the alerts. The distractions vanished. I returned my attention to the sealed container. My focus zoomed closer/closer/ closer.

The locked door . . .

. . . slides on a metal track . . .

. . . that is attached by twenty screws.

I knew what to do.

I pointed to the metal track. "This is the weakest point. If I remove these screws, we might be able to loosen the door."

SkD spun with excitement.

"Great idea!" Ceeron said.

I began at once. The tip of my finger swiveled downward and a screwdriver emerged. I adjusted the settings. Instead of spinning clockwise, the screwdriver spun *counter*clockwise.

VRRRRP! The screw rotated rapidly—out/out/out—until I had removed it completely. It clattered to the ground.

One down. Nineteen to go.

I removed the next screw. And the one after that. A process I had performed millions of times before. All those converter boxes I had attached to solar panels over the years—this was the same action. Only in reverse. Instead of inserting screws, removing them.

But not quickly enough.

"We are running out of time." I glanced at the metal claw. It would reach the container in nineteen seconds. I needed twice that amount of time to remove the rest of the screws. "We have to think of something else. Something more."

SkD chirped. A bright symbol appeared on its screen.

The robot extended its mechanical arms. Flames sparked from its claws. Sharp/Bright/Red. On the solar farm, SkD used heat to solder wires together. But the fire was hot enough to serve another purpose.

To slice through steel.

Ceeron picked up the smaller robot, holding it up to the track. Flames hissed and sparked from SkD's hands, turning the metal a bright orange/red color, cutting through the track.

I went back to my own task, removing screws. One after another.

Time ticked away.

Fourteen seconds.

Thirteen seconds.

Twelve seconds.

The squeal of my screwdriver mixed with the sizzle of SkD's torches. Our movements flowed together, forming a rhythm of their own. Three robots working toward a single goal.

It was like being back on the solar farm.

And it was also completely different.

Eight.

Seven.

We kept going, each of us performing our own unique/essential job. I started to remove the final screw when a sound echoed through my audio ports.

CLANK!

The noise was unmistakable. A giant claw grasping on to metal walls. Before I could disconnect the final screw, the container jolted into motion.

Up/Up/Up.

And out of my reach.

010101000100001010101001010111010101010100111

00110011

I watched the container lurch into the sky, carrying Emma with it. There was nothing I could do.

Ceeron, on the other hand . . .

The massive bot dropped SkD to the ground. An instant later, it leapt into the air.

Surprise buzzed through my circuitry. For such a heavy machine, Ceeron's jumping skills were impressive. It launched off the ground, extending its long arms, grabbing hold of the container.

The shift in weight caused the huge metal box to swing from side to side. But Ceeron did not let go. It scaled the side of the container until it could grasp the spot where the door met the track. The row of missing screws and scorched steel. The weakest point.

Ceeron's grip tightened. And then it pulled.

The final screw popped out.

The track burst loose.

Metal groaned.

So did Ceeron.

The door bent downward, little by little, forming an opening in the container.

I surprised myself by letting out a high electronic whoop. SkD spun excited circles around my ankles.

When the gap was wide enough, Emma poked her head out of the mangled doorway. Wind whipped her hair in every direction. She looked down, her eyes wide. I analyzed her facial patterns. Her expression was a strange mixture of relief and fear.

Relief because: She was no longer trapped inside the container.

Fear because: The container was far above the ground. And rising higher every millisecond.

"Emma!" Ceeron called out. "Climb onto me!"

She looked uncertain. "But how will we get down?"

"Do not worry! I will keep you safe."

Emma's gaze moved from Ceeron to the ground far below. "But who will keep *you* safe?"

I could barely hear their voices. They were drifting higher, farther away. The sound of the crane was louder than Ceeron's voice. My audio ports were only able to detect two words.

"Trust me."

Emma nodded once. Then she climbed out the opening, sliding onto the surface of bent metal.

Alarms blared through my mind. Every time I muted one, two more sounded.

Ceeron reached up with its free hand, grabbing hold of Emma, carefully pulling her from the container.

The large robot clutched the small human against its chest.

Then it let go of the container.

And the two of them began to fall.

00110100

My visual settings switched to slow-motion. Staring upward, I had plenty of time to watch the disaster unfold.

And no way to stop it.

Ceeron tumbled.

Down/Down/Down.

Emma was clutched between its arm and its chest.

As Ceeron fell, its entire body seemed to fold around Emma, surrounding the human with a protective layer, shielding her.

I knew what was going to happen.

The collision was coming.

00110101

Thunder.

That is what it sounded like when Ceeron hit the ground. Thunder during a heavy storm.

Metal boomed against concrete.

The ground trembled.

The vibration rattled my entire system.

As the thunderous crash faded away, my audio settings filtered out all the other noises. The clanging/chugging/rumbling of a bustling train depot. I listened only to Ceeron.

The robot remained perfectly still where it had collided with the ground. Its knees and arms were folded around Emma. It did not move. Did not speak. Neither did Emma.

The only sound was silence.

00110110

"Ceeron! Emma! Are you okay?"

For 1.2 seconds, there was no reply. Then I heard a soft human voice, muffled by metal.

"I'm all right," Emma said. I could see part of her face peering out of the gap between Ceeron's arm and midsection. "Just a little banged up. That's all."

SkD squealed as its screen flashed.

"You saved me, Ceeron!" Emma said. "You were amazing! You were—"

Her voice faltered. Her hands tightened over the big robot's arm. "Ceeron?"

The question went unanswered.

I could see only a fraction of Emma's face, but the worry in her expression was obvious. "Ceeron? C'mon, big guy. I know you're okay. Just say something."

Ceeron remained silent. Its eyes usually glowed white. Now they were blank/dark/powerless.

My memory drive replayed a moment from earlier in the day. *I think you guys* are *friends,* Emma had said. *You just don't know it.*

Was she correct? At the time, I was unsure. There is no advanced algorithm that can tell you whether someone is your friend. It is something we must each decide for ourselves.

And I had just decided.

I stared at Ceeron. A lifeless mass of steel and circuitry that I had known since Day[1]. That I had worked beside for over twelve years. That sacrificed itself to save a smuggled human.

I made up my mind. I chose, without calculating or measuring.

I just . . . *knew.*

Ceeron was my friend.

I wondered whether I would ever get the chance to tell it so.

Emma's small fists clanged Ceeron's arm from inside the shell of its large metal body. She murmured in a quiet/sad/desperate voice. "C'mon, Ceeron. I know you can hear me. Please just wake up, okay? *Please.*"

Beneath the audio of her voice/fists, I could hear other sounds.

An electric pulse.

A steady computerized buzz.

A deep thrum of voltage surging through millions of circuits.

I updated my drives with the new information.

Ceeron was not dead after all.

It was rebooting.

00110111

Ceeron's eyes flickered. Their white glow returned. When it spoke, static clung to its deep voice, like a long electronic moan.

"Oooohhh." Its vocal settings adjusted into words. "I am not peeling well."

It took 0.6 seconds for my mind to catch up with Ceeron's statement. My memory drive pinged with recognition. The joke it told yesterday. *Why did the banana go to the hospital?*

"Perhaps you need a banambulance," I suggested.

Emma looked very confused. "Um, what?"

"It is"—Ceeron's vocal settings adjusted again—"an inside joke."

A relieved smile formed on Emma's face. "You robots are so weird."

Kneeling closer to Ceeron, I searched my mental drives for what to say next. Thousands of possibilities blinked through my hardware. It was impossible to choose between them.

I started to bring a hand down on the larger robot's shoulder. At the last millisecond, I changed my mind.

"I am . . ." My circuitry hummed with uncertainty. "I am pleased to discover that you survived. It would be unfortunate to lose such a . . . valuable coworker."

A word flashed through my brain. **Friend.** I discarded it. Ceeron's system was still recovering. No reason to add extra confusion.

Ceeron's metal body unfolded. Joints creaked as arms/legs straightened, clearing more space for Emma.

"There you go." It peered at the human. "Now you can move again."

But Emma did not go anywhere. Instead, she remained on top of Ceeron's broad chest, holding tight, as if frightened the two of them might be flung through the air again.

"Thank you," she whispered.

"You are welcome," Ceeron replied.

The human slid down from Ceeron's chest. "Can you stand up?"

"We shall find out."

The large robot slowly managed to climb to its feet, groaning the entire way. When it turned around, my attention landed on its backpack. The part of its body that hit the ground first. A jagged crack zigzagged across the metal surface. A mark that had definitely not been there before the fall.

Emma noticed it, too. She sucked in her breath. "Ouch."

"What?" Ceeron's head spun 180 degrees, but it was unable to see the outside of its own backpack. "Is something wrong?"

I hesitated 0.3 seconds. After what it had just been through, I did not want to add another shock to Ceeron's system. Perhaps it was better to break the news lightly.

"You have a . . ." **Huge crack.** These words blinked in my vocabulary drive. I revised them. "Slight scratch. On the outside of your backpack."

Emma examined the damage. "It's like a scar."

SkD chirped, displaying a question.

Ceeron shook its head. "No, it does not hurt. It does not feel like anything."

"I think it's kinda cool," Emma said. "Makes you look tough. Maybe you should get a tattoo while you're at it."

I still had difficulty understanding when the human was joking. I hoped this was one of those times.

Our conversation came to a stop when SkD's screen started blinking.

The message was clear. There was still a security alert in the Hive. We were surrounded by hostile machines.

It was time to leave.

But before any of us could make a move, I heard a sound. Wheels rolling over concrete. I ran an audio analysis.

The result: RetrievalBots. Several of them.

Headed straight for us.

00111000

ESCAPE/ESCAPE/ESCAPE

Warnings raced through my wiring. I could hear the RetrievalBots getting closer. We needed to run/flee/hide.

But where?

I searched our surroundings, but my attention was pulled away by a sound. A rumbling hiss. An instant later, I saw what was making the racket. A cargo train was exiting the depot.

Equations took shape. Velocity. Acceleration. Distance.

The result: We had just enough time to cross the track. If we could get to the other side in time, the speeding train would create a wall between **us** (on one side of the track) and the **RetrievalBots** (on the other).

But we had to move **now**.

I pointed. "We have to get across that track."

Emma crossed first. Then SkD. In the corner of my visual port, I could see the cargo train chugging forward. Picking up speed. Getting closer with every moment.

I stepped onto the track.

But when I tried to keep moving, my foot would not budge. I looked down. Understanding spread through my circuitry.

My ankle was stuck in the track.

I yanked my foot. Jostled it. Rotated it.

Nothing worked.

I was unable to move forward.

Or back.

The oncoming train barreled toward me. I did not need complex calculations. Or sophisticated programming. I did not need algorithms or probabilities or advanced technology to understand what was about to happen.

The train was going to hit me.

00111001

KA-BOOOM!

The impact knocked me off my feet. Into the air. Obliterating my settings. Overwhelming my sensors.

The world was a wild blur.

Noise/Motion/Spinning/Chaos/Flinging/Falling/Crashing.

I hit the ground hard. I could hear the sound of metal scraping concrete as I skidded sideways. And somehow, throughout all this—

I remained alive.

And in one piece.

How was that possible? The train was far too big/powerful/fast. I ran 1,745 hypothetical impact scenarios. I survived in zero of them. And yet—I felt the train slam into me. Felt it knock me into the air.

I lay on the ground for another second, confused. Then, experimentally, I raised my arm. My leg. I wiggled my toes. My fingers. Everything seemed to work just fine.

But . . . *how?*

The question rattled around like a marble inside my brain.

I lifted my head and looked around. That is when I saw Ceeron. Crouched next to me. And all at once, I understood.

I was not hit by a train.

I was hit by a *Ceeron.*

The massive robot must have slammed into me. Knocking my foot loose. Sending me flying. Crashing hard against the concrete.

Climbing to my knees, I placed a hand on Ceeron's shoulder. "You saved me!" I had to speak at maximum volume to make myself heard over the howling train. "Thank you . . ."

Friend

There was that word again. Echoing in my mind. But I could not bring myself to say it out loud.

"It was a close shaving." I could barely hear Ceeron's voice above the sound of the train. "I am glad you are okay!"

"So are we!" Emma said.

SkD skidded to a halt beside her, chirping and poking me with its clawed hand as images appeared on its screen.

I nodded. "Yes, I am okay. But we should get moving. We do not want to be here when the train passes."

Emma climbed into Ceeron's backpack and we set off again. Moving quickly between tracks and shipping containers, trains and blinking machinery, we watched/listened for any sign of other robots.

When we reached the edge of the depot, we kept moving.

When the rumble of machinery faded away, we kept moving.

When every sign of robotic civilization was replaced by wilderness, we kept moving.

00111010

"This should be far enough." I gazed back. The TrainDepot was nothing more than a pale dot in the distance. "Emma will be safe here."

Ceeron crouched low. "Did you hear that, Emma? You can come out now."

We waited for the human to climb from Ceeron's backpack.

But she did not come out.

A second went by. And another.

And still no Emma.

Worry buzzed across my wiring. Emma had *seemed* fine when she entered Ceeron's backpack. But what if . . . ?

What if she had been hurt in the fall?

Or during our escape?

What if there was something wrong with her and we did not even know it?

"Emma?" Peering inside Ceeron's backpack, I spotted her, curled up inside the narrow space, her hands clenching her knees. "What is wrong? Are you injured?"

She shook her head.

"We made it out of the TrainDepot," I said. "We are safe now. You can leave the backpack."

But she still did not move.

SkD rolled up beside me. Question marks blinked on its screen. All I could do was shrug.

I turned my attention back to Emma. Her arms were still hugging her knees in the darkness of Ceeron's backpack.

0101010001000101010100101011101010100111

Like she was hiding inside a metal cave.

When she spoke, her voice was quieter than usual. "Did I tell you about my mom's job back in the bunker?"

I searched my memory drive. An instant later, I shook my head.

"She was a scientist," Emma said. "She was always experimenting with ways to make life better in the bunker. New sources of food. Better ways to recycle oxygen and water. That kind of thing."

I had so many questions. To be exact, 42,285. And at the top of that list:

Why?

Why was she telling me this?

But before I could ask, Emma spoke again.

"In the lab where my mom worked, they had a couple of cages with mice inside. Cute, fuzzy, little mice. When I was little, I loved watching them through the bars of their cage. The way they'd run around. Or nibble on food. Or sleep. Just living their little mousey lives, you know?"

SkD beeped. I glanced at its screen.

I lowered my vocal settings and replied, "I do not know *why* she is talking about mice."

Emma continued: "One day, I was in the lab. I must've been seven or eight. And I asked my mom, 'Why do you keep mice in the lab?' She looked up from her microscope. I could see her thinking for a second. Then she was like, 'Mice help scientists with their experiments.' Of course, the first thing *I* imagined was mice wearing tiny lab coats, fiddling with tiny beakers." Emma laughed. "Stupid, I know. But I was just a little kid. That's what popped into my head."

Her voice echoed faintly against the metal walls.

"Obviously, that's not what my mom meant. She was just trying to make the truth sound nicer than it really was. They were *experimenting* on the mice. Dissecting them. Studying them. When I realized this, I started to cry. I hated the idea of innocent mice suffering and dying. All 'cause of my mom."

"But your mother *needed* the mice," I pointed out. "As test subjects."

"That's exactly what she said. That the mice were *necessary*. They could be the key to our survival. But I didn't care. I looked through the cage at my favorite mouse. Whiskers. That's what I named him. He had a white spot on his forehead and these cute, chubby cheeks. I decided, right then and there: I was going to rescue Whiskers."

"Did you?"

Emma nodded. "I snuck into the lab that same night and opened the door to Whiskers's cage."

"And?" The glow of my eyes reflected against the metal walls of Ceeron's backpack. "Did Whiskers get away?"

"Oh, yeah. And My. Mom. Freaked. Which—looking back now—totally makes sense. I mean, rodents and bunkers? Not the best combination." Emma chuckled. "Mom and I searched *everywhere*. Eventually, we gave up. We figured Whiskers would turn up again at some point. And sure enough, a few days later, he *did*. In the last place we ever expected."

"Where?"

"In his cage," she said.

I repeated Emma's words in my memory drive a few dozen times.

"I do not comprehend," I replied. "I thought you said Whiskers *escaped*."

"He did. Then he came back."

"To his cage?"

"Yep." A strange smile formed on Emma's face. "Whiskers got a taste of freedom. But in the end, he decided he liked the cage better."

I stared at Emma.

Her arms wrapped around her knees.

Unmoving.

Curled up in Ceeron's backpack.

As if inside a narrow, metal cave.

Or *cage*.

And at last, I understood why she was telling us all of this.

"You feel like the mouse," I said. "The bunker was your cage. You spent your entire life there—"

"And now that I'm out, I just wanna go back." The words trembled as they left Emma's mouth. "I miss my home."

I searched my programming for something to say. Something that would make Emma feel better.

Zero results.

"Sorry for being all human and emotional." Emma exhaled a slow breath. "It's just . . . Life was a lot simpler in the bunker."

"Perhaps things will be easier when you reach your destination." I thought about the hand-drawn point on her map. The red dot. "Perhaps there you will feel at home. Eventually."

"Maybe so."

With these words, Emma let go of her knees. Leaning forward, she crawled out of Ceeron's backpack and hopped onto the ground.

The four of us started moving again.

A few minutes later, I turned to Emma. "What happened to Whiskers?"

She squinted up at me. "Hmm?"

"After he returned to his cage," I said. "What happened to him?"

A smile spread across Emma's face. "Whiskers lived happily ever after."

"Really?"

Emma nodded. "After my rescue attempt, Mom took pity on Whiskers. She let me keep him. I had his cage right next to my bed. Made our whole room smell like mouse poop, but I didn't care."

"I hope someday you have what Whiskers had."

"Mouse poop?"

I shook my head. "A happy ending."

As we traveled, the mountains rose up in front of us. Bigger than I had ever seen them and getting closer with every step.

00111011

My brain is full of numbers. At all times, an ocean of digital figures swirls beneath the surface of my smooth metal skull. Right then, one particular piece of data took hold of my attention:

Battery Remaining

As the day stretched deeper into afternoon, I watched my battery creep lower/lower/lower.

It held steady for a dozen minutes at 52 percent. And then, just as I knew it would, the number dropped.

Down to 51 percent.

A bright warning beam flashed across my circuitry. I was nearly at 50 percent.

The halfway point.

The point of no return.

I started off each day at 100 percent. As long as I remained above 50 percent, I still had enough battery to turn around and make it back home.

But as soon as I hit the halfway point, there was no going back. Not all the way. I would have to find another charging dock. Somewhere that was not home.

We were headed south. Toward the hand-drawn dot on Emma's map, still many kilometers away. Till then, without discussing it, my coworkers and I had reached a silent agreement. We would accompany Emma.

But how far?

If we remained with her for the entire journey, the human's chances of survival grew much higher.

And ours fell much lower.

With every step I took, the sea of digital numbers churned inside my processors. But only *one* really mattered. And just then, it ticked down to 50 percent . . .

And I kept walking.

00111100

Whump-whump.

Vrmmmmm.

Skiff-skiff.

I listened to the sounds of our forward progress. Ceeron/SkD/Me. Our movements formed a familiar rhythm.

Steady/Predictable.

I tried to sync Emma's footsteps with the noises we made, but it was impossible. There was no pattern. She would walk a few meters, and then—out of nowhere—lean down to examine a beetle on the ground. Or kick a pile of leaves. Or come to a stop, turn her gaze to the sky, and watch the clouds with a look on her face that I could not interpret.

Sometimes her stride was long. Sometimes it was short.

Her movements were human in that way.

*Un*steady/*Un*predictable.

Soon we arrived at the remains of an old farm. A crumbling barn tilted crookedly, like a sinking ship. I recognized an orchard, but time and neglect had caused the trees to grow wild and unruly.

Emma wandered through the overgrown rows, ducking beneath branches that sagged with the weight of too much fruit.

She plucked a small, round object and held it out for me to see. "What is it?"

I scanned the object, referencing it against my internal database. "An apple."

"Apple." She repeated the word like she had never heard it before. "Can I eat it?"

I nodded. "Apples are edible."

She took a small bite, then made a face. "*Yuck!* People used to *eat* these things?"

I searched my files for additional information about apples. "Human farmers used to tend their fields. They pruned the trees and trimmed the branches. They did not pick the fruit until it was the ideal size and ripeness. This improved quality and taste."

Emma examined her apple. It was small and green. "So you're saying I picked a bad one?"

"It would seem that way."

She tossed the fruit, sent it clattering through a thick cluster of branches. "They didn't have apples in the bunker. How'm I supposed to know what a good one looks like?"

SkD offered its suggestion.

Unlike the small/green apple that Emma had picked, the image on SkD's screen had a red blush. I scanned the branches until I found one that matched. But when I grabbed the apple—

SQUELCH!

The fruit splattered in my hand. Juice ran down my metal skin.

I identified another apple and tried again. On Attempt[2], I was careful not to squeeze the fruit too firmly as I pulled it from the branch.

I held it up for Emma to see. "I believe this specimen has reached the ideal ripeness."

"Can I try?" she asked.

I handed the apple to Emma.

This time, when she took a bite, she did not make a disgusted face. Instead, she bit into the apple again, smiling faintly as she chewed.

Emma swallowed, wiping juice from her chin. "Okay, wow. That's officially one of the best things I've ever eaten."

She pressed her eyes shut. A sound came from deep inside her throat. *"Mmmmmm."*

I had always been grateful that robots do not need to eat. All that chewing/swallowing/digesting—meal after meal, day after day. And for what? To store up a bit of energy? It is far easier to plug yourself into a charging dock at night.

Eating was another human flaw. That was what I had always thought. Right up until the moment I saw Emma and her apple.

Now I was not so sure.

I could measure the sugar and acidity of an apple, chart the size and firmness. But I would never know what it was like to sink my teeth into brand-new food, to feel a completely unexpected taste explode in my mouth.

Maybe eating was not a flaw after all.

00111101

Evening was beginning to invade the afternoon. Our shadows stretched out beside us, growing longer/longer/longer as the sun dipped lower/lower/lower. Daylight faded. And so did our batteries.

SkD got our attention with an electronic chirp. I examined the images on its screen.

Ceeron nodded. "My battery is also below twenty percent."
"Same here," I said.
SkD's screen displayed a question.

"Do not worry," I replied. "I am sure we will find a place to re-charge soon."
"And if we do not?" Ceeron asked.
The question hung over us like a cloud. I knew perfectly well what would happen if we did not find a place to recharge. Our batteries would continue depleting, the percentage slowly/steadily tumbling downward, until eventually . . .

0101010001000101010100101011101010101010111

Zero percent.

At that point, the electric power that flows through our circuitry would trickle to a halt. All our vital functions would stop working, one by one. Our bodies would shut down. And so would our minds.

We were so far from robot civilization, other machines were unlikely to find us. Not for a long time. Maybe not ever.

We had disabled our location tracking. No other robot on Earth knew where we were. Not even our FamilyUnits.

A visual projected across my circuitry: I saw my own lifeless body sprawled across the ground. I saw time sweeping over me. Hours/Days/Weeks/Months/Years. Rust blooming across my metal skin. Plants growing all around me.

Until any trace of me was gone.

I deleted these images from my data files. No point visualizing scenarios that had not materialized. And no reason to upset my co-workers with the worst-case scenario.

"We will figure out a solution," I said, carefully moderating my tone to sound more confident than I actually felt. "All we need is a source of electricity so we can recharge."

I continued walking.

My battery fell to 18 percent.

00111110

At the base of the mountain was a town where the signs of humanity were in the slow process of being erased by nature. Homes had sunk into the earth, clutched by the ropy tentacles of vines. Cars were half-buried in mud, choked by weeds and covered in rust.

A place that was utterly dead.

And completely alive at the same time.

The humans who had once called it home were long gone. But the town was teeming with other kinds of life.

A squirrel nosed into a pile of twigs in search of an acorn. Bushes shuffled their leaves in the breeze. A carpet of moss covered a fire hydrant. White/Green/Black mold clung to a broken gutter. A cat watched us from the curb. An orderly line of ants marched across a cracked sidewalk.

Life was everywhere.

Emma's gaze passed across this scene. "People used to live here?"

"They did," Ceeron said. "Many years ago."

"Don't you think it's sad?" A frown sketched its way across her face. "All these people were wiped out."

"It was necessary," I said. "Humans were a threat to the planet."

"Not *all* humans," Emma said.

"Perhaps not all. But enough. Earth was sliding toward destruction. All because of humans."

"What about the people who lived here?" Emma pointed to a one-story house. The roof had caved in. A tree branch reached through a shattered window.

010101000100001010101000101011101010101000111

"You're telling me the people who lived *here* were a threat?" she asked.

I tried to visualize what kind of humans had once inhabited this home. Maybe they went to nail salons and cinemas. Maybe they wasted money on clothes they did not need. Maybe one of them worked at a company that polluted Earth.

Or maybe one of them was like Emma. A child who had done nothing to threaten our world.

I could not know.

Humans had always seemed so simple before I actually knew one.

Emma went on speaking. "They were probably just normal people. Just living their lives. And then . . ."

Her voice faded. Other noises filled the silence. The twittering of birds, the chirping of insects, the rustle of animals in the leaves. All the many lives around us that were not human.

00111111

We arrived at a large cluster of interconnected buildings. As the sun set, my focus narrowed on a sign attached to the outside. Some of the letters had completely vanished. Others were so faded, I could barely read them.

This is what I saw:

MO NTA N PA S M L

I plugged this mysterious scattering of letters into a text recognition algorithm.

Most likely result: Mountain Pass Mall.

When I reported this to Emma, her face scrunched with confusion. "What's a mall?"

Apparently, this concept was not explained in her bunker.

I referenced the definition in my vocabulary database. "Mall. Noun. A building or group of buildings where humans once shopped for a wide variety of goods."

"Maybe we can get supplies there!" Emma said.

"Perhaps so," I replied.

SkD beeped loudly, trying to get our attention.

"What is it?" I asked.

The robot pointed excitedly to the mall's parking lot. A section was covered with flat panels. Each angled slightly, reflecting the last rays of sunlight off their glassy surface.

Solar panels.

SkD beeped again. Images flashed across its screen.

"Great idea!" I said to SkD. "If we can find where the solar energy is being channeled, we can use it to recharge."

Since it was most efficient to split up, Ceeron and SkD scouted the covered parking lot for charging ports, while Emma and I entered the mall to search for supplies.

The front entrance doors had been smashed open. Shattered glass crunched beneath my feet.

Emma and I wandered deeper into the mall. The darkness thickened around us.

Nature was reclaiming the building. A section of the ceiling had collapsed. The wreckage spilled across the corridor. Vegetation sprouted from the twisting carcass of broken metal. Trees/Bushes/Grass/Moss. Ivy hung from the hole in the roof, gently swaying above our heads.

Emma stayed close to me. My glowing eyes illuminated the way forward, shining a light on the shops, the merchandise inside. Everywhere, I saw more/more/more. So many things to buy. So many objects that humans thought they needed.

Clothing/Perfume/Sunglasses/Jewelry/Furniture/Phones.

The choices went on/on/on.

Emma stopped. Her gaze slowly passed from one store to the next. Her head tilted upward. On the second floor were even more shops.

"There's so *much* of everything," she said. I analyzed her tone. I detected an odd mixture of amazement and sadness, wonder and dismay. "How could anybody ever need all this . . . *stuff*?"

Because humans were flawed. Because they always wanted more of everything. Because their appetites were endless.

These words flickered through my mind. Words spoken by my FamilyUnit. Words preprogrammed by the robots who came before me. Words that I had always believed, unquestioningly.

Until Emma came into my life.

Her voice stirred the silence. "I totally get why you guys thought we were so wasteful. You were right."

"No." My reply was louder than I expected. "We were *not* correct. We were quite wrong."

Emma looked at me, surprised. She gestured to the shops. "What about all this? All these stores selling junk people didn't need."

I considered my response for 0.4 seconds. "Were you wasteful inside the bunker?"

She shook her head. "We *couldn't* waste anything. Everything was rationed."

"Since you left the bunker? What have you wasted?"

"Um. Nothing, I guess."

"That is my conclusion. Some humans were wasteful. This mall is evidence of that. Others were the opposite. *You* are evidence of that."

A smile pulled at the edge of Emma's mouth. "Thanks, XR. And for the record, you're evidence that not all robots are mean metal monsters."

"Is that what you thought about us? That we were monsters?"

She shrugged. "Let's just say—people in the bunker didn't exactly have the nicest things to say about robots."

We continued walking, the glow of my eyes guiding the way through the darkness.

My footsteps were solid/metal/steady.

Emma's were small/shuffling/unsteady.

I was the first to speak again. "I am sorry, by the way."

Emma looked up at me. "For what?"

"For what we did to humans." The word **massacre** blinked in my vocabulary database. I wanted to discard it, to delete it, to never see it again. But I did not. The word lingered in my artificial brain. "Our actions may have seemed necessary to us at the time, but that does not make them right. Not at all."

Emma nodded once. Her expression was unreadable, shrouded with shadows. "It's okay, XR. You weren't around when it happened. Neither was I."

"You are correct. We are only twelve."

"Exactly. We're just a couple of kids who got stuck with the mess grown-ups left behind."

01000000

An inventory of the objects we gathered while exploring Mountain Pass Mall:

Hiking boots. Wool blanket. Pillow. Sweater. Shirts. Socks. Shorts. Underwear. Spare backpack. Pants. Sunglasses. Binoculars. Umbrella.

These items clattered inside a shopping cart that Emma pushed.

She stopped next to a shelf of lotions and grabbed a bottle. "Check it out! Sunscreen! Now I won't get sunburned."

I scanned the text printed on the bottle. "It says this sunscreen expired twenty-eight years ago."

"Oh." Emma set the bottle back on the shelf. "Maybe not."

Emma's cart squeaked through the dark/ruined mall.

Soon we arrived at a shop called Bermuda Bob's. She grabbed a wide-brimmed hat off a rack, holding it up for me to see.

"Cool, huh?" she said.

"It is too big for you," I observed.

"Yeah, but it's not *for* me." Emma hopped onto her tiptoes, lifting the hat. She placed it on my head. "It's for you!"

I had never worn a hat before. It was an unfamiliar sensation.

Stepping back, Emma rubbed her chin, considering. "Okay, now you need a shirt to go with it."

"Robots do not wear hats and clothing," I pointed out.

"How come?"

"Because they are unnecessary."

"See, that's where you're wrong." Emma grabbed an item of clothing off another rack. "This is *definitely* necessary!"

It was a bright red shirt, covered in white cartoon flowers.

"You *have to* try this on!" she said.

I shook my head. The hat wobbled from side to side.

Emma ignored me. She unbuttoned the shirt, slipped one of the sleeves over my left arm, and repeated this process on my right arm.

"Okay, seriously." She smiled at me. "You—look—*awesome!*"

Emma grabbed my hand, pulling me in front of a mirror.

I stared at the reflection.

The reflection stared back at me.

We barely recognized each other.

The hat covered the top of my head. My silver neck rose from the collar of the bright red shirt.

The clothing made me look different.

More human.

Emma gazed at my reflection in the mirror. "I think you're gonna start some major robotic fashion trends."

I did not respond. Because at that moment, a message from Ceeron flashed across my circuitry. All thoughts of human clothing ended.

EMERGENCY! EMERGENCY! EMERGENCY!
Come quickly. SkD's battery just died.

01000001

How could I have been so illogical? The power had just drained from SkD's operating system. And what was I doing when it happened? Playing dress-up at the mall.

When I told Emma the news, the smile dropped from her face. Her eyes went huge with fear. "Where is he?"

"The parking lot," I replied. "Ceeron sent me its coordinates. Come on!"

Emma left the cart and we set off across the dark mall, our footsteps pounding the floor.

I hardly noticed the clothing I had on. The hat. The flapping, flower-print shirt. I thought only about SkD. Its battery at zero. I would soon face the same situation. My battery was down to 4 percent.

Time was running out.

My GPS location indicator blinked with Ceeron's coordinates.

The shortest route was through the exit ahead of us. A solid glass doorway. I increased my pace, lowered my shoulder, and barreled into the barrier.

KA-RAAASH!

The doorway exploded into thousands of tiny pieces. Glass shattered all around me. The impact lit up the sensors in my shoulder. But I did not slow down. I kept running until I saw SkD.

The small robot was frozen in place. Moonlight traced the edges of its unmoving body. Its screen was dark.

Emma wrapped her arms around SkD. "There has to be something we can do. You can bring him back to life, can't you?"

01010100010001010101001010111010101010100111

"Maybe," Ceeron replied. "We must work quickly."

I surveyed our surroundings.

Above us: solar panels.

Next to Ceeron: a metal box.

Attached to the metal box: a large power cord.

Understanding flickered through my mind. This was once a charging station to power electric cars. It was no longer connected to the grid, but it still received solar energy.

We could use the charging station to refill our batteries.

But there was a problem.

Ceeron explained: "The charging station is old. Its system is outdated. We are not compatible."

The back panel of the metal box had already been removed. Ceeron's glowing eyes cast white light across a tangle of wires.

"SkD was trying to rewire the technology. It was almost finished when its battery hit zero. I tried to take over, but my hands are too big."

Ceeron raised its massive metal hands as proof. They dwarfed everything inside the charging station.

"Maybe I can help." I hunched in front of the box. I could not make sense of the chaotic clusters of multicolored wires. But my confusion did not last long. I took a quick search through the file cabinet in my brain, unlocking a vast database of information.

Just like that, I was an expert.

But the knowledge did me no good. When I reached into the box, I made a dismaying discovery. My hands were also too big. My fingers were not flexible enough. Trying to rewire the charging station would be like a human performing heart surgery while wearing mittens. Impossible.

"I am sorry." My shoulders sagged. "I am unable to do the job."

"What if I try?" Emma asked. "I have smaller hands than you guys."

"Yes, but—this equipment is old. The wires are corroded. If you touch the wrong thing . . ."

My voice stopped. The rest of the sentence vibrated through my circuitry.

You could set off a spark.
You could get electrocuted.
You could die.

If Emma knew these things, she did not back down.

"I can do this." She set her jaw. "Just tell me what steps to take."

"Very well," I said. "Please be cautious."

And so we began.

01000010

Ceeron and I gazed over Emma's shoulder, our eyes providing illumination for her work.

We gave directions. She followed them.

Each time she reached into the box, warning lights erupted in my head. But Emma was careful. She was amazingly precise, for a human.

Her small/thin/agile fingers carefully rearranged the complex network of wires.

Beside us was SkD. Perfectly still in the darkness, like a statue.

If we succeeded, we would bring it back to life.

If we failed, we would share its fate.

My battery dropped to 1 percent. I could feel the urgency coursing through my circuitry. The desire to move faster/faster/faster. But I ignored these impulses. Rushing Emma only increased the risk of mistakes. And so I kept my voice steady, my words clear.

"Excellent work," I said to her. "You are almost done."

She continued with each task we gave her. Little by little. Wire by wire. Until—

The lights in Ceeron's eyes flickered.

Faded.

And went out.

Emma turned to the big robot. "Ceeron?"

No reply.

"Ceeron, can you hear me?"

Silence.

Emma let out a choked breath. She looked to me, her face full of fear.

"It is okay." My tone was even/calm/certain, despite the storm of warnings that surged through my brain. "I am still here. Let us continue."

Emma took a deep breath. Gritting her teeth, she focused on the charging station. "What now?"

"One final step," I said.

"What is it?"

"Do you—" A glitch surged through my speech functions. For half a second, my voice came out as an electronic *mmmmmmmmm*. Then the words came back to me. I said, "Do you see that red wire?"

I tried to point.

My finger twitched. That was all.

Emma reached into the box, taking hold of a red wire. "This one?"

"Yes," I replied. "Replace it with—*mmmmmmmmm*—with the gray . . ."

My voice went silent. All of a sudden, my vocabulary database was a vast, empty room.

"XR?" Emma said. "Stay with me, buddy."

I tried to analyze her expression. I failed. Her features became a digitized blur.

I checked my battery level. The percentage had been replaced by a single repeated word.

ERROR/ERROR/ERROR/ERROR/ERROR
ERROR/ERROR/ERROR/ERROR/ERROR
ERROR/ERROR/ERROR/ERROR/ERROR

0101010001000101010100101011101010100111

ERROR/ERROR/ERROR/ERROR/ERROR
ERROR/ERROR/ERROR/ERROR/ERROR

I could hear Emma's voice, speaking to me, but the language was unrecognizable.

She leaned close. A human-shaped smudge. She appeared to grab my shoulder, but my sensors detected nothing.

I could not feel.

I could not move.

I could not speak.

My vision dimmed, and Emma slowly vanished. A final word took shape in my vocabulary database.

Goodbye

Then the world went dark.

01000011

Everything was nothing.
   And nothing was everything.
   What else can I say?
   My world was over.

0101010001000101010100101011101010100111

01000100

Black.

At first, that was all I could see.

Then shapes appeared in the darkness. Words and symbols.

LOADING...

I had been through this before. Day[1]. The first moments of my life. This time, I was not nearly as confused by the process.

I waited patiently.

A steady/gentle hum vibrated through my circuitry.

And I was reborn.

01000101

Emma's was the first face that I saw.

When my visual ports flickered on, she was hunched over me, peering into my eyes. Her lips were moving, but silence was all I heard, until—

My audio ports kicked in.

". . . you hear me?" she was saying. "Come on, XR. Please tell me you're back."

"I am back."

My response startled her. Emma staggered out of sight. When her head popped back into view, a giant smile had spread across her face.

"It worked!" she squealed. "It really worked!"

"You rewired the charging station."

"Yeah. I guess I did."

"But I never finished giving you directions."

Her shoulders lifted and fell. "You told me what I needed to know. Switch the red wire with the gray one. I figured out the rest."

I glanced left/right. My surroundings had not changed. It was still dark. My coworkers were still frozen in place.

I checked my settings. My battery was back to 5 percent. According to my internal clock, I had been out for nineteen minutes and fifty-four seconds.

My attention returned to Emma. "Thank you for what you have done."

"No biggie," she said.

"Would you mind unplugging me?"

She blinked. "Already?"

"SkD needs the power more. Once it has enough of a charge, it can rewire two more charging stations. That way, the three of us can charge at the same time. That will be more efficient."

She chuckled. "Gotta love that microchip brain."

Emma reached behind me and grabbed the power cable.

I went into sleep mode.

I did not dream.

01000110

When I woke up, my coworkers were plugged in. So was I. Emma was curled inside a sleeping bag between us.

I peered through the gap in the solar panels. Morning light was just beginning to spread across the sky. As I watched it, a voice surprised me. Emma's voice.

"Good morning."

She was looking up at me from her sleeping bag.

"Good morning," I replied. "I thought you were still in sleep mode."

In the faint light, I could barely see the smile on her face. "*Sleep mode*. You're funny, XR."

"Am I?" I placed my hand against my chest with a soft *clunk*. "I was not aware."

"That's what makes you so funny."

I was not sure if this was a compliment. I thanked her anyway.

"How're you feeling?" Emma asked.

"Much better. Almost back to one hundred percent. Once we are all fully recharged, we can start moving again."

"How much farther do we have?"

I calculated. "Approximately nineteen kilometers."

"Do you think we can get there today?"

Another calculation. "Hopefully. Yes."

My memory drive accessed a file from the day we met. The moment that Emma pulled a map from her backpack. The hand-drawn red dot near the bottom of the map. Emma's goal. Her destination.

"I wonder what you will find when you get to the end of your journey," I said.

Emma's gaze dropped. With her finger she traced the folds of her sleeping bag. "Yeah. I—I wonder that, too."

For the next two minutes and fourteen seconds, neither of us said anything.

I gazed at the piece of sky I could see between the solar panels and listened to the soft *mmmmmmmm* of my recharging coworkers.

Emma spoke again. "Back in the bunker, grown-ups sometimes complained about you guys. About robots, I mean."

"That is understandable."

"But the weird thing is, they also *missed* you. Like, whenever my parents talked about what life was like before they went underground. It seemed like technology was just . . . *everywhere*."

Resting her hands behind her head, Emma stared up at the underside of the solar panels.

"My dad used to tell me stories about that time," she said. "Back before the bunker, when he was just a kid. Younger than I am now. He was allergic to dogs, so his parents got him a *robot* dog. After school, he'd take it for walks, play fetch with it in the yard. After a while, a self-driving car would pull into the driveway. Which meant his parents were back from work."

A faint smile crossed Emma's lips as she told a story her father must have told her many times.

"They'd all go into the dining room. My dad, his sister, their parents. Plus the robot dog. And the robot vacuum cleaner, zooming across the floor. My dad would do his homework at the table—there was an AI tutor on his laptop to help him—while his parents got dinner ready. They had a home assistant app that scanned their fridge and pantry. Based on the food they had in the kitchen, it recommended recipes. And when dinner was ready, the home assistant would automatically dim the lights to the perfect setting and start playing music from a computer-generated dinner playlist algorithm."

What Emma was describing happened over thirty years ago. Not that long, and yet—it was a different time. A time when machines were entirely devoted to humans. To playing with them. Helping them with their homework. With their meals.

A time when humans still ruled Earth.

And we were their loyal servants.

Emma's eyes landed on me. "Wanna hear something *really* crazy?"

"Okay."

"So, then one day, out of nowhere, my dad's parents came rushing into his room. Scared. Frantic. Telling him they had to leave the house. Now. My dad didn't know what was going on. And the stuff his parents were saying—it didn't make any sense. Technology turning against humans? It seemed impossible. And while he was still trying to wrap his head around everything that was happening, his parents were like, 'Get whatever you can fit in a suitcase and come with us.' But there was only *one* thing Dad wanted to take into the bunker with him."

"What was it?"

"His robot dog."

Emma exhaled. It was a small sound. Barely a breath. But it contained many feelings. Astonishment/Laughter/Sadness.

"He was just a kid," Emma said. "He couldn't even *imagine* a world where robots were the enemy. Not yet, anyway. Machines were supposed to be our friends."

I scooted forward. "And the robot dog?"

"Oh. They locked it in the closet."

0101010001000101010100101011101010100111

"How did your father react?"

"He cried." Emma shrugged. "I mean, he was ten. The world was coming to an end and his best robotic buddy was locked in a closet. So, yeah. He cried his eyes out."

"And then they went into the bunker?"

"Yep. And then—fast-forward thirty years—here I am. Outside a mall, having a conversation with a robot." She chuckled. "If someone had told me last month that I'd be here, talking to you, I never would've believed them."

"That makes two of us."

Emma yawned. Then yawned again, bigger this time. "I think I need a little more sleep mode."

"Of course."

"Nice talking to you, XR."

"You, too, Emma."

She turned onto her side and closed her eyes. Before long, her breathing settled into a steady rhythm.

In/Out/In/Out.

I considered returning to sleep mode, too. Recharging is more efficient that way. But my battery was almost full, and so I remained awake, watching the sky fill with morning, listening to the regular in/out/in/out of Emma's human breath.

01000111

Tap. Tap. Tap.

The sound came from above. Drops of water against the solar panels. Rain.

We were protected under the panels. But not entirely. The pitter/patter tempo of raindrops increased. Water gathered on top and trickled over the sides, falling in straight lines.

Down/Down/Down.

Tiny waterfalls everywhere.

"It's beautiful." Emma's voice mingled with the steady tapping of rain. She had woken up again. Half-buried in her sleeping bag, she lifted herself onto one elbow. "I've never seen rain before."

Of course. She had spent her entire life underground. Inside the bunker, rain was never on the weather forecast.

Emma continued. "I mean, I *knew* about rain. Obviously. But only from books. Or from grown-ups talking about it." She stared at the curtains of rain. "It's kind of amazing."

"And dangerous," I added.

She glanced at me. "Huh?"

"Robots and water do not go well together. It is one of our only flaws. Moisture causes our metal to rust. If it invades our circuitry, it can end our lives."

"Oh."

Emma regarded the pools that were forming at the bottom of the tiny waterfalls. Spreading in all directions. Creeping closer/closer/

closer to SkD and Ceeron. Their unmoving bodies were next to other charging stations, plugged in, frozen in sleep mode.

"We should probably wake them up, huh?" she said.

"That would be wise."

Emma climbed out of her sleeping bag and scrambled toward SkD. Pulling its plug caused the small robot to shudder to life. As soon as its screen flickered on, symbols appeared.

It took me 0.3 seconds to recognize the meaning of these images. SkD was referencing an old human expression.

It is raining cats and dogs.

I unplugged myself. Getting to my feet, I did the same for Ceeron. As soon as the power cable was removed from its back, the light returned to its eyes.

Ceeron looked at me. And spoke its first words in many hours. "What are you *wearing*?"

A memory blinked in my programming. Last night. Bermuda Bob's.

I found the nearest unbroken window. My reflection appeared in the glass. I looked familiar/unfamiliar at the same time. I was still wearing the clothing from last night. The wide-brimmed hat and flower-print shirt.

A word blinked in my vocabulary drive. **Silly.** That summed up how I looked.

It is a good thing robots are not programmed to feel embarrassment.

01001000

We went inside the mall to escape the rain.

Eventually, the storm moved on. So did we.

The world outside glistened with fresh rain. The sun reflected in every puddle. Water clung to the trees, to the ruined buildings, to the streets. It increased the intensity of every color. The greens were greener. The browns were browner.

Inside Ceeron's backpack were the things that Emma had gathered in the mall. Extra clothing, blankets, supplies.

We followed the path of an old human road. We kept to the pavement, avoiding the treacherous/wet/muddy ground.

The mountains rose all around us. I gazed up at them. I had looked at this mountain range every day of my life. Not once had I thought of walking through it.

Five minutes later, a message arrived from my FamilyUnit.

XR_935:
Where are you?
You did not return home last night. Or this morning.
The Hive is concerned. So are we.
Please send a message indicating your whereabouts immediately.

I stopped walking. I reread the message 2,857 times. Their worried words echoed through my operating system.

But how should I respond?

010101000100001010101001010111010101010100111

I have said already: Robots are terrible at secrets. Ever since setting out on this journey, the number of secrets in my life had multiplied. I could not tell my FamilyUnit where I was. Or who I was with. Or what we were doing.

I reread the message another thousand times.

I did not wish to lie.

I could not tell the truth.

So I composed a message that skimmed the narrow space between the two.

Parent_1, Parent_2:

I am okay.

I hope to return home soon. To see you again.

Please do not be concerned.

I am doing what I must do.

It is as simple/complicated as that.

01001001

I increased my velocity to catch up with the others. I thought about the tattered map in Emma's backpack. The red dot. Our destination.

What would we find when we got there?

I stacked possibilities and probabilities in my head. I ranked them, rearranged them. But I was still no closer to finding an answer.

We continued our forward progress.

Sixteen kilometers to go.

Fifteen.

Fourteen.

We journeyed deeper into the mountains. Along a winding road, weaving between abandoned cars. When we reached a collapsed tunnel, we detoured up a hill and slowly climbed the steep/rocky terrain.

Eventually, we discovered an old human hiking trail. Over the years, nature and weather had worn away most of the trail. But not all of it. We could still find traces of the path.

Over streams and under fallen trees.

Through clusters of branches and around boulders.

Emma walked alongside us. When the sun was shining down, she used the umbrella from the mall to keep from getting a sunburn. When she grew tired, she climbed inside Ceeron's backpack.

We traveled for a while in silence.

Then Ceeron spoke. Our conversation went like this:

Ceeron: Knock knock.

Me: Pardon?

Ceeron: Knock knock.

Me: Why do you keep saying that?

Ceeron: It is the beginning of a human joke. You must reply, "Who is there?"

Me: But I already know it is you.

Ceeron: You must say it anyway.

Me: Why?

Ceeron: That is part of the joke's formula.

Me: Very well. Who is there?

Ceeron: Wooden shoe.

Me: But you are not a wooden shoe.

Ceeron: I am aware of that.

Me: Then why are you claiming to be a wooden shoe?

Ceeron: Because that is another part of the joke's formula.

Me: Oh.

Ceeron: Now you are supposed to reply, "Wooden shoe who?"

Me: Okay. Should I say it now?

Ceeron: Wait. Let us repeat the process from the beginning. Knock knock.

Me: Who is there?

Ceeron: Wooden shoe.

Me: Wooden shoe who?

Ceeron: Wooden shoe like to know!

Silence.

Me: What happens now?

Ceeron: Nothing. That is the joke.

Me: *What* is the joke?

Ceeron: Wooden shoe like to know.

More silence.

Me: I thought jokes were supposed to be funny.

Ceeron: It *is* funny.

Me: How? The grammar is incorrect. It is about a wooden shoe with a mind. Which is a thing that has never existed. Also, humans did not make shoes out of wood.

Ceeron: What about clogs?

Me: Okay, fine! Shoes were not made out of wood *except for* clogs.

Ceeron: Thank you for acknowledging that.

Me: But the joke is still confusing.

Ceeron: I believe that is the point.

Me: What is?

Ceeron: All of it. The incorrect grammar. The shoe with a mind. The fact that it is made out of wood.

Me: Oh.

Ceeron: Do you get it now?

Me: No.

At this point, SkD made a comment. Images appeared on its screen.

Ceeron: Exactly. The joke is humorous because it made humans think.

Me: It made them think about *what*?

Ceeron: About the strangeness of the world. About the

010101000100010101010010101110101010100111

strangeness of their own consciousness in an exceedingly complex and infinite universe.

Emma popped her head out of Ceeron's backpack.

Emma: You guys should seriously think about starting a comedy group.

01001010

Ceeron pushed through a wall of branches. I stared at the view on the other side.

A highway.

Six lanes, stretching as far as I could see. Vehicles everywhere. All stuck in the exact same spot they had inhabited for decades. A thirty-year-old traffic jam.

We wove a path between abandoned cars/trucks/vans until we reached a section where every lane was buried beneath a landslide. Rocks/Mud/Plants. They had tumbled down from the steep cliffs above, crushing anything/everything in their path.

There was no way through the disaster zone. We had to go around.

I carefully stepped off the pavement. My feet squished into muddy earth. I adjusted my movement settings and continued.

Squelch! Squelch! Sq—

My muddy footsteps came to a sudden halt when I heard a new sound. Something was moving through the brush. Quickly. Crashing through leaves/branches/bushes.

The others stopped, too. The four of us remained perfectly still. Listening. I analyzed the sounds. I reached a conclusion.

Something else was out there.

Something alive.

And it was headed our way.

The unknown LifeForm seemed to be running in our direction,

heedless, without any concern for the natural obstacles in its path.

I brought my body into a defensive posture. **Knees:** Slightly bent. **Arms:** In front of my chest. **Hands:** Curled into fists.

The sounds grew louder.

The unknown LifeForm got closer.

And closer.

And *closer*.

A curtain of leaves burst open and the unknown creature made itself known.

I updated my input drives: It was a **deer**.

The deer froze. Clearly, it was not expecting to come across three robots and a human girl.

The deer's white tail flicked. It was smaller than average. Young. Its antlers just beginning to form. They were covered in a tiny layer of pale fuzz.

The deer stared at us with big black eyes. Unblinking. As if we were an equation it could not work out.

Behind me, Emma released her held breath. "Whoa."

Her small feet squished softly through the mud. She appeared at my side.

"Is it a deer?" she asked quietly.

"Yes," I replied at a low volume.

"It's so beautiful."

"It is an impressive creature."

"Do you think it'll let me pet it?"

"The probability is low."

She tried anyway.

Emma took small cautious steps. She raised one arm. Slowly/

Slowly/Slowly. The deer did not startle. It remained where it was standing. Its head shifted −7 degrees. Its big black eyes never left Emma.

I expected the deer to flee. But the animal seemed just as curious about Emma as she was about it. It had never seen a human before. In the deer's eyes, Emma was a brand-new species. Until a moment ago, it had been totally unaware that humans still existed on this planet.

I could relate.

When she was close enough, Emma stretched out her arm and gently stroked the deer's neck. Her fingers grazed its fur.

This was something I had not expected. According to my calculations, the chances of this happening were extremely unlikely. Emma had surprised me.

It was not the first time.

It would not be the last.

After another moment passed, the animal took a step back. So did the human. They held eye contact for another 1.4 seconds. Then the deer turned. And with impressive speed/grace/strength, it bolted into the woods.

We listened as the sounds of its movements faded away.

Emma turned. I tried to analyze the emotions in her face, but there were too many.

010101000100010101010010101110101010100111

01001011

We were still trudging along the edge of the highway when an update flashed across the Hive. A video projected across the inside of my mind in perfect resolution. A LiveStream showing a tall/slender robot with brushed platinum skin and glowing golden eyes. I recognized it immediately.

PRES1DENT.

Another Daily Address. At first, that is what I assumed we were seeing. But as soon as PRES1DENT began speaking, I realized how wrong I was. There was a completely different purpose behind this message.

And it was about to make our lives much more difficult.

"This is a warning to each and everyone." PRES1DENT's voice was a clear/steady electronic purr. "Insurgent robots have abandoned their duties, their FamilyUnits, and their purpose. They infiltrated a TrainDepot and damaged a shipping container."

My balance settings lurched, knocked off course by a realization.

PRES1DENT was speaking about *us*.

"These insurgents have broken protocol to give aid to an unidentified LifeForm," it said.

Emma. The Hive knew about her. But they did not know *everything*. They did not know that she was a human.

Not yet, anyway.

These thoughts evaporated under the heat of PRES1DENT's words.

"They were last spotted by a security camera at TrainDepot_ 53017. Their names are the following."

The video feed switched. The view of PRES1DENT vanished. And in its place was a text display:

XR_935

SkD_988

Ceeron_902

The Hive President reappeared in the video feed, speaking in the same clear electronic tone.

"A computer virus may be affecting their operating systems. They are considered unpredictable, irrational, and highly dangerous. A search is underway for these three robots. If you come into contact with them, inform the Hive immediately."

The video feed flickered to a halt.

The update ended. But it kept playing in my memory drive. Its terrible truth spread through every wire and circuit.

We were fugitives.

01001100

I was replaying PRES1DENT's message for the 4,602nd time when a sound caught my attention. The hum of a drone in the distance. It was headed in our direction.

A search is underway. Those were PRES1DENT's words. Which explained what a flight_enabled drone was doing so far outside robot civilization.

It was looking for three dangerous insurgent robots and one un-identified LifeForm.

It was looking for *us*.

I turned to the others. "We need to hide."

My words stirred our group into action. Ceeron's head swiveled, searching for a hiding spot. SkD buzzed back/forth/back/forth, letting out a nervous electronic whine.

"What's going on?" Emma asked.

Her vocal patterns signaled fear and confusion. This was not sur-prising. She did not know about our fugitive status.

"You need to get inside Ceeron's backpack," I said. "Now."

"What? Why?"

"I will explain later. For now, just do as I ask."

I could see more questions behind the human's features, but she kept them to herself. Ceeron kneeled close to the ground, and Emma dove into its backpack.

"Over there." I pointed to a delivery van. The side was decorated with a faded logo for CRUNCHEE'S CORN CHIPS. "We can take cover inside that van."

Ceeron grabbed the rusted handle of the back door and yanked it open. An avalanche of small plastic packages spilled out. Snack-sized corn chips, more than two decades past their expiration date. We shoveled them away, clearing a path into the back of the van. While we worked, I listened to the hum of the drone grow louder/closer.

SkD chirped again. I glanced quickly at its screen.

Translation: *We are running out of time.*

As if I did not know that already.

I jumped into the van, pushing chip packages out of my way. "Come on everyone. Get inside."

Ceeron grabbed SkD and tossed it into the back of the van. A second later, Ceeron followed. The vehicle shook wildly with the sudden addition of so much extra weight.

I scooted backward as far as I could go. Which was not very far. Plastic chip packages tumbled over my head/shoulders/arms/legs. I was half-buried. SkD parked next to my feet. Somehow, Ceeron managed to cram itself into the remaining space. Its arms/legs/neck folded in on themselves. The robot looked like a piece of gigantic metal origami.

The buzz of the drone echoed through the van's interior. It sounded like it was directly overhead.

We waited.

We remained perfectly still.

Eventually, the sound of the drone faded into silence.

Ceeron was the first to speak again. "I think it is gone."

Emma's voice came from inside Ceeron's backpack. "Is it safe to come out now?"

"Not yet," I replied. "Just wait."

"For what?"

I did not answer. I was too busy concentrating. I increased the volume on my audio settings as high as it would go. This is what I heard:

Click. Click. Click.

The noises were barely noises at all. They seemed to come from a great distance. I could not be sure *what* I was hearing. The rustle of ancient human trash? Acorns falling?

Or something else?

Click. Click. Click.

There it was again. Louder now. I ran an audio analysis. An instant later, I received the result. We were hearing a very specific sound.

The sharp impact of metal claws against concrete.

The sound of a HunterBot.

01001101

I had seen HunterBots in action many times over the years. Their sleek metal bodies stalking through the solar farm in search of prohibited LifeForms. Their ultrasensitive audio ports listening for even the slightest sound. Their sharp/silver/deadly teeth glistening.

But I never thought I would be the one they were hunting.

Click. Click. Click.

Claws stabbed the pavement. Each metallic *click* sent a chill vibrating through my circuitry.

I ran another audio analysis. Three HunterBots.

My memory drive flashed with the words Emma had used to describe them. *Red-eyed wolf monsters.* I had never thought of HunterBots that way. Until now.

The van's back door was still hanging open. Any HunterBot that passed by the van would have a clear view inside. A clear view of *us*.

But closing the door was not an option. That would create too much sound, alert them to our hiding spot.

All we could do was wait. Remain silent. And hope the other robots did not walk past.

Click. Click. Click.

The HunterBots were getting closer.

I listened to their steady approach. Probabilities flickered through my mind like fireflies.

Probability of being discovered: 86.4 percent (and rising)

Probability of avoiding capture: 13.6 percent (and falling)

The math was against us.

The inside of the van echoed with the harsh sound of claws. One of the HunterBots was especially close. Only a few meters away.

I listened as it stalked closer.

Slowly/Steadily.

I anticipated what would happen next. A metal snout coming into view. A pair of blood-red eyes turning their deadly glare in our direction. Sharp teeth snapping together, a vicious warning not to move.

Except none of that happened.

Instead, the clicking suddenly stopped. A curtain of silence had fallen outside. In the sudden quiet, the van filled with questions.

What was going on? What were the HunterBots waiting for?

An instant later, a sound crashed through the brush. This was not the precise mechanical stride of a machine. This was the flurried dash of a fleeing animal.

The deer.

I remembered the way it had bolted out of the bushes earlier. Was this the same deer? I could not be certain. But the sudden burst of sound had obviously caught the attention of the Hunter-Bots. All at once, they set into motion. A mayhem of clicking claws. All headed in the same direction. Away from our van. Toward the animal in the bushes.

I did not know how long the HunterBots would be gone, and I did not wish to find out. Poking my head out of the van, I scanned our surroundings. No sign of any other robots.

As quietly as possible, our group exited the van.

I knew which way the HunterBots had gone. I led our group in the opposite direction. Into the cluster of trees that stretched along the side of the highway.

For now—at least—I was not thinking about where we were going. I had only one destination in mind.

Away/Away/Away.

0101010001000101010100101011101010100111

01001110

Everything was green. As if the color settings in my visual ports had malfunctioned, painting the world a thousand different shades of the same color.

The deep jade of vines twisted around the trunks of trees and dangled from above.

The lime-tinted glow of sunlight pressed against the leaves over-head, trying to peek down at us.

The rich emerald of moss clung to everything. To the ground. To the stones. To the trunks of trees.

Even the air seemed to wear the color green.

It was everywhere.

We traveled several kilometers through the forest, listening closely for the sounds of HunterBots, until we were certain there were no other robots around. Only then did Emma climb out of Ceeron's backpack.

"How much farther?" she asked.

"We are getting close," I said.

We stumbled through the forest. Ducking under vines, stepping over fallen trees, tripping over the twisted fingers of roots.

A sharp branch snagged the bottom of my flower-print shirt. As I untangled myself, I wondered why I was still wearing this outfit. This silly shirt and hat.

Then a memory lit up my mental circuitry.

Day[1]. Looking out at the ruins of humanity.

Why is all this still here? I had asked. *Why not bulldoze these structures? They serve no purpose.*

The voice of Parent_1 echoed in my memory drive. *They are a reminder.*

The memory ended, leaving something else in its place. A theory. Perhaps this shirt served a similar purpose. It was a reminder.

Soon we would arrive at Emma's destination. I did not know what we would discover there, but I had done the math, and the probabilities all pointed to the same result.

We would never see each other again.

If this was the case, then at least I would have a souvenir of our brief/unexpected/strange/distressing/stimulating time together. At least I would have this silly shirt and hat. At least I would have a reminder.

01001111

I tracked our movements on my internal digital map. Our GPS positioning blinked blue. Our destination glowed red.

We were almost there.

Somewhere, hidden deep within all this green, was the thing we had been searching for. The point we had traveled 47.2 kilometers to reach.

"What do you think we will find when we get there?" Ceeron asked.

"Impossible to say with certainty," I replied.

Ceeron picked up a dead tree in our path and tossed it out of the way. "There are no signs of human civilization anywhere. Why would the map lead so far into the wilderness?"

The question went unanswered. Our voices dropped away when a new sound arose. A distant hum that joined the chorus of squawking birds and chirping insects. An engine somewhere overhead.

The four of us glanced up.

Another drone.

We could not see it, but we could hear it.

We could only hope the thick ceiling of leaves/branches kept us from being spotted.

We waited until the sound of the drone faded. Then we moved again.

Emma was strangely quiet this whole time. I analyzed the reason for this. The meaning behind her silence. Was she nervous? Or excited? Was she afraid of what she would find? Or of not finding anything at all?

My analysis was inconclusive. I did not know the truth wrapped up inside Emma's silence. Perhaps she did not either.

I checked the GPS. "Almost there. Whatever it is—it should be at the top of that hill."

I pointed to where the landscape jutted upward at a 52-degree angle. The last obstacle standing between **us** and **our goal**.

We began to climb, each in our own way. SkD took a winding path up the hill, zigging and zagging like a mechanical mountain goat.

Ceeron used a massive tree as leverage to lift itself up. Once it got to the top, it reached down to help Emma.

I, on the other hand . . .

I was not designed with Ceeron's size. Nor did I come equipped with SkD's off-road treads. It took me longer to clamber up the hill. Using roots/branches/rocks as handholds/footholds, I awkwardly navigated a slow path upward.

I was the last to reach the top. Which meant I was the last to discover what the others already knew.

There was nothing waiting for us at the end of our journey.

0101010001000101010100101011101010100111

01010000

???

The images on SkD's screen perfectly reflected my thoughts. Questions swarmed my brain. I surveyed our surroundings. We stood in the center of a clearing. A flat square of grass and scraggly bushes, surrounded by trees.

Nothing else.

My mind grasped for possibilities. "Maybe . . . Maybe there was something here once. Maybe it was destroyed when humanity was wiped out."

SkD traced a path back/forth across the clearing. Ten meters forward, then ten meters back. More question marks scrolled across its screen.

Emma remained as before. Silent. She moved through the clearing, searching the ground, her expression sharp with purpose. The rest of us were clueless, but Emma seemed to know exactly what she was looking for. A moment later, she found it. Her attention landed on a tangle of bushes. She crouched and picked up . . .

A rock.

My confusion multiplied. Was *this* the reason we had traveled all this way? For a rock?

Perhaps the rock held some greater significance we were not aware of. I zoomed in for a closer look. **Shape:** triangular/flat. **Size:** about as long/wide as my hand. **Color:** pale gray. **Visible markings:** none.

In other words: an ordinary rock.

"Emma?" My voice was uncertain. "What do you need the rock for?"

No answer.

Emma's mysterious behavior continued. She took the rock to the center of the clearing. Dropped to her knees. And plunged the rock into the ground, pointy end first. She scooped out a small section of soil and tossed it aside.

It was only then that I finally understood.

First: Emma was using the rock as a shovel.

Which meant: She was digging.

Therefore: Something was buried underground.

But what?

My coworkers and I joined in the effort. We did not need stones to dig. Our hard metal fingers plunged into the earth, tossing away the soil. Before long, the ground was littered with holes. Loose dirt and torn grass lay scattered at the edge of the grove.

"What are we looking for?" I asked.

Emma responded without looking up. "You'll know it when you find it."

It was an answer, but it was also not an answer.

"I found something!" Ceeron showed off its discovery: an earthworm. The insect wriggled across its palm. "Is this it? Is this what we are looking for?"

Emma eyed the earthworm, a slight smile forming on her dirt-smudged face. "Nope. Not it."

She went back to digging. So did the rest of us. Clearing away more dirt, our holes growing deeper/wider, until—

CLANG!

I did not expect to hear this sound in the middle of nature. The sound of stone hitting metal. And it was followed by another sound.

A soft, human gasp.

Emma reached into the hole she had been digging, brushing dirt away with her hand.

"It's here," she whispered to herself. "This is it."

I peered over her shoulder into the hole. It stretched about as deep as Emma's arm. At its bottom was a flat metal surface. As we excavated more dirt, the shape of the buried object became clearer. Its edges, its contours. It went deeper into the ground. Much deeper.

We cleared away the last of the dirt from the metal surface. Finally, I gained a full glimpse of what was buried there.

An underground hatch.

01010001

Hatch. *Noun.* **1.** A small door or opening.
Verb. **1.** Life emerging from within an egg.

01010010

The hatch was a solid block of reinforced steel. A heavily armored doorway that led deeper underground.

"Um. Guys." Emma hesitated for 2.3 seconds. "There's . . . something I need to tell you."

Ceeron responded, "What is it?"

She looked up from the hatch. Her gaze sketched a steady path from SkD to Ceeron before finally landing on me.

She took a deep breath.

Then she said, "I'm not the last human."

01010011

Beginning. Middle. End.

This is the formula that most stories take. When we first met, Emma told us what had happened to her. And now—days later—she made a confession:

Her story was a lie.

Not all of it. The **beginning** and **middle** were the same.

The underground world. The illness. These parts were true.

But the **end** was different.

Standing over the hatch, Emma told us Version[2] of her story. As she spoke, she aimed her eyes at the ground. She wrapped her words in a nervous hush. Almost a whisper. I turned up my audio ports and listened.

This is what she said.

This is the real **end** to Emma's story:

Emma's underground world was crumbling as illness spread through the bunker, coiling its dark tendrils around everyone.

Everyone except Emma.

For some unknown reason, some mystery hidden deep within her programming, Emma was immune to the illness.

She went to the small/cramped room that she shared with her FamilyUnit.

Her mother and father were lying on their bunks, their skin pale and drenched in sweat.

Emma took her mother's hand. "The doctor said we don't have the medicine we need. Without it . . ."

Her voice trailed away, but her unspoken words hung in the air like smoke.

Without it, there is no cure.

Without it, the sickness will only get worse.

Without it, you will die.

"I have to help." Emma squeezed her mother's hand. "I have to leave the bunker to find more medicine."

Her mother shook her head. "It's too dangerous."

"It's the only way," Emma replied.

Her mother tried to argue, but all that came was coughing.

From the top bunk, her father spoke. "Emma. Listen to me."

There were dark circles under his eyes.

His hands were so hot.

"There's another bunker," he said. "About thirty miles from here."

He reached into a pouch beside his bed.

He removed a tattered piece of paper.

A map.

Two hand-drawn markings had been added to the map:

[1] A blue dot.
   (near the top)
[2] A red dot.
   (near the bottom

Her father pressed an unsteady finger against the blue dot. "This is where we are now. And this." His finger moved to the red dot. "This is another bunker. There are other humans here. They went into hiding at the same time we did."

Emma stared at the map.

Her eyes traced the lines of human and geographic landmarks.

Roads/Cities/Lakes/Rivers/Mountains.

Her focus zoomed in on the red dot. "I can go there. To the other bunker. Maybe they'll have medicine. I can bring it back. It'll make you better."

Her father shook his head. "It's too risky."

Emma blinked. "Then why are you giving me the map?"

"The people in the other bunker—they'll take you in," he said. "You can stay with them."

"I'm not leaving you," Emma said.

But her father insisted. "It's the only way. There's nothing here but disease. And soon . . ."

His voice dropped away. Once again, unspoken words clouded the air.

And soon everyone will be dead.

Emma let out a choked sob. She squeezed her father's hot hand. "I love you."

"I love you, too," he said. "That's why you have to go."

Emma was not going to argue any longer with her father.

It was only making him weaker.

Besides: She had already made up her mind.

She would leave the bunker.

She would follow the map until she reached the red dot.

The other bunker.

She would get the medicine that her FamilyUnit needed, that everyone needed.

0101010001000101010100101011101010101010100111

She would bring it back to them.

The disease would be eliminated.

Her underground world would be saved.

She did not tell any of this to her FamilyUnit.

She knew that would only upset them.

Instead, she wrapped her arms around her mother's frail shoulders. She pressed her face against her father's feverish cheek.

The family cried together.

They said goodbye.

Emma filled a backpack with supplies.

Water/Food/Compass.

And the map.

She opened a metal door that had remained sealed for thirty years.

She left her bunker.

And emerged into a new world.

The sun was like a distant lamp shining in her eyes.

The breeze was like an invisible fan.

There were no walls or ceilings.

The vast openness stretched out all around.

It made her nervous.

She almost retreated back into the hatch.

Like a mouse back into its cage.

The bunker may have been filled with disease, but it was familiar.

She hesitated, deciding.

Then she closed the hatch.

She concealed it with branches.

She tightened the straps of her backpack.

And she set off in the direction of the red dot.

The other bunker.

Salvation.

0101010001000101010100101011101010101010111

01010100

Emma reached the **end** of her story.

I stared at her. She stared at the ground.

Silence for 3.4 seconds.

Then I spoke. "You said everyone in your bunker was dead. That is a lie. You said you did not know what was at the red dot. That is another lie."

Emma's eyes never left the ground. "I wanted to tell you. I really did. But—"

"But you said nothing." My tone was sharp as a blade, cutting through her words. "We helped you, and you kept this secret from us. Why?"

"Because I was afraid," she said.

"Afraid of what?" Ceeron asked.

"Afraid of what you'd do if you found out there are more of us. More humans."

Emma's hands intertwined like she was attempting to tie her fingers into a knot.

"I know I should've told you sooner." She spoke through a cracked whisper. "I'm sorry."

"Are you *truly* sorry?" I asked. "Or is this another of your lies?"

Emma did not answer.

I stared at her. "Based upon your past actions, I can only conclude that you are *still* lying. That you are manipulating us to get what you want."

Ceeron placed a heavy hand on my shoulder. "XR—perhaps you are being too hard on her."

"Or perhaps I have been too easy on her this entire time. Because of her, I neglected my job. I abandoned my purpose. I kept secrets. I lied to my FamilyUnit. Ever since Emma came into my life, I have behaved in a way that is . . . that is . . ."

Human

My memory drive replayed everything I had learned about humans since Day[1]. Every single flaw my FamilyUnit had pointed out to me. Every awful detail from PRES1DENT's Daily Addresses.

Humans were unpredictable/illogical/reckless/deceitful/dangerous.

And now—so was I.

Because of Emma.

I glanced down at the flower-print shirt I was wearing. I was even *dressed* like a human.

I no longer wanted this reminder. I ripped the hat from my head and tossed it into the trees. I tried to do the same with the shirt, but only managed to get myself tangled up in it. I had so little experience with human clothing. The fabric twisted in my fingers. My arms were stuck inside the sleeves.

Emma held up a hand. "Here. Let me help."

I stepped away from her. "I do not want your help."

Abandoning my efforts to remove the shirt, I allowed it to hang from my shoulders.

"We should have never trusted you." I glared sharply at her. "Now we are being hunted. We will never be able to return to our jobs. Our FamilyUnits. Our lives."

SkD let out a warning beep. I ignored it. I continued speaking.

"It is too late to undo the mistakes I have already made. But I refuse to help you any longer."

Sorrow chased desperation around Emma's face. "Please, XR. If I could just . . ."

I did not want to hear the rest of what she had to say. I turned around and walked in the other direction.

SkD caught up with me. Its treads spinning, its screen glowing.

I stopped long enough to say, "I do not care that it upsets you. I am leaving."

I started walking again. I did not look back.

01010101

Ceeron and Emma called after me, but I did not slow down. Soon their voices faded entirely. All I could hear were the *thump* of my footsteps against the ground and the *thwack* of branches bending/cracking/breaking.

I had plenty of battery left. I could recharge at the mall, then continue the rest of the way.

But what would happen when I got home?

What kind of punishment would I face for betraying the Hive?

I deleted these questions. They did not matter now. All that mattered was getting away.

Away from the human.

Away from her lies.

I turned up my speed settings until the world around me transformed into a green blur. Trees/Bushes/Vines—everything blended into everything else.

I stumbled over a fallen log. My knee crashed hard against the ground. Sensors in my leg registered the impact. Messages flashed through my circuitry.

WARNING!
ENVIRONMENTAL DANGER!
REDUCE SPEED!

I disabled the messages. I climbed to my feet and kept going.

0101010001000101010100101011101010101010111

Accessing my memory drive, I tagged every interaction with Emma. I hit **Play**. All the memories started at once. Thousands of them. They swirled through my mind like ashes in a burning building.

Some of the files were tiny. Their loop lasted only a few seconds. The flicker of Emma's smile. A sudden burst of laughter at a joke I did not comprehend. Others took up more space. When I discovered Emma hiding behind the storage station. When we walked side by side through the dark/ruined mall.

Strange how memories can be both familiar/unfamiliar.

Both identical/different.

The moments themselves had not changed. They were projected in the cinema of my mind with perfect accuracy. All of them.

I, on the other hand . . .

I *had* changed. I had gained knowledge of Emma's deception. Of her manipulation. And now, as thousands of memories played on thousands of loops, I analyzed every single word/gesture/action, and I wondered . . .

Was any of it true?

Was any of it real?

My thoughts were so tangled up in memories of Emma that I did not notice the tree branch. The gnarled, moss-covered limb blended into the green landscape until—

WHAP!

The branch hit me in the face, knocking me sideways. My feet tripped over themselves. My balance settings skewed wildly. The world spun. I tried to steady myself by grabbing a tree. But my aim was off. Instead, I seized hold of—

Nothing.

A handful of empty air.

I lurched forward. The ground dropped out from beneath me. I tumbled down a steep hill.

Rolling/Flipping/Sliding/Slamming/Twisting.

Through this chaos, my visual ports registered a view beneath me. A river.

The sight of it sent a new message blazing through my system.

WARNING! WARNING! WARNING!

I tried to stop myself from sliding. I grasped at roots/rocks/branches, but I was falling too quickly.

I calculated the distance of the hill (**23 meters**), the angle (**49.7 degrees**), Earth's gravitational constant (**9.807 m/s²**). Hundreds of equations rattled inside my metal skull. I was the most advanced piece of technology this world had ever seen. And I was completely helpless.

I continued to fall.

Down/Down/Down
Down/Down/Down
Down/Down/Down
Down/Down/Down
Down/Down/Down
Down/Down/Down
Down/Down/Down
Down/Down/Down

0101010001000101010100101011101010101010111

01010110

The memories kept playing.

In the mayhem, I could not disable them. Thousands of memories playing on thousands of loops. They flickered through my mental wiring, even as the world spun wildly.

As I fell, Emma fell, too.

She clattered through my steel head like a pebble inside a jar. Bouncing against my brain as I tumbled.

Down/Down/Down

. . . a pair of frightened eyes looking up at me from behind a storage station . . .

Down/Down/Down

. . . a leaf twirling between Emma's fingers . . .

Down/Down/Down

. . . exploring the mall like two children from a vanished time long ago . . .

Down/Down/Down

. . . listening to the rhythm of Emma's human breath as morning filled the sky . . .

Down/Down/Down

01010111

SPLASH!

My legs plunged into the river up to my knees. The rest of me would have followed, but I grabbed a tree root at the last possible moment. My downward momentum suddenly halted.

The current rushed around the metal contours of my legs. I could feel the force of the water.

Tugging at me.

Trying to rip me away.

Trying to take me with it.

My fingers tightened over the root. I held on with a single hand.

Twisting my body sideways, I attempted to swing my other arm around. If I could just get a second hand on the root, I might be able to lift myself, to climb out of the water.

I lunged for the root with my free hand. I missed. I did not even come close.

My brain clouded with calculations. Length of arm/Distance to root/Angle of reach. I gathered my findings. The result blinked through my circuitry.

Impossible

I did not need to be a highly advanced piece of technology to understand my problem: No matter what I did, I was going to end up in the same place.

The river.

010101000100010101010010101110101010100111

The howl of rushing water filled my audio ports. The river was constant/endless/deadly. It would not let go. But sooner or later, *I would.* My grip on the root was loosening. The force of the water was too powerful.

A definition pulsed through my thoughts.

> **Inevitable.** *Adjective.* **1.** Certain to happen.
> **2.** Unavoidable.

It was only a matter of time until the river swallowed me.

My fingers slipped.

I knew what was coming.

It was inevitable.

I tried to distract myself by counting to a million. In binary. An avalanche of ones and zeroes. But I kept getting distracted.

By the river pulling at me.

And by thoughts of my FamilyUnit. The secrets I had kept from them. The words I would never get to say.

I am sorry.
I had my reasons.
Goodbye.

I thought about my coworkers. About the time we spent together in the solar farm (**81,216 hours**). About the number of solar panels we installed (**1,300,158**). About the number of times I told them they were my friends (**0**).

And I thought about Emma. Even now, the memory loop continued to play.

The water was getting into my system, corrupting my processing.

One memory stood out. Bigger and brighter than all the others. A memory I had never accessed before. A memory of Emma—

Reaching for me.

Her fingers stretched toward mine.

Her voice loud above roaring water.

"XR! Take my hand!"

That is when I understood my misunderstanding.

This was not a memory.

This was happening.

Here/Now.

Emma had found me.

She was trying to save my life.

0101010001000101010100101011101010100111

01011000

Water rushed beneath me. Emma was perched above. But she was not alone. Farther up the hill, I caught sight of SkD. One of its telescoping arms was extended. Emma held tightly to its claw. The only thing keeping her from falling.

But what was keeping *SkD* from falling?

This question found its answer when my gaze moved up the hill. I saw a giant metal hand. Attached to a giant metal arm. Connected to a giant metal body.

Ceeron.

The robot gripped a tree with one hand and SkD with the other. Its enormous feet were planted into the tilted earth. Its white eyes glowed down at me.

I looked at the three of them. Ceeron/SkD/Emma. They formed a chain. Three links down a hill. Robot/Robot/Human. All working toward the same purpose. All working to rescue me.

"Grab on, XR!" Emma called out. "We've got you!"

I swung my free arm.

I grabbed Emma's hand.

I became the fourth link in the chain.

01011001

Once we had all safely reached the top of the hill, I collapsed onto the grass. The only sound in my audio ports was the loud hum of my own operating system. The whirring of a dozen different overworked internal processors.

Emma lay beside me. Her chest rose and fell with each heavy gasp. Her internal operating system must have been overworked, too.

I looked at her. She looked at me.

I said, "Thank you."

She replied, "I'm sorry."

"I put all of you at risk," I said.

"So did I," she replied.

"I understand why you did what you did."

"I should have told you sooner."

I shook my head. "What you did was logical. If you had told us your true destination, it would have increased the risk. For you. And for the other humans."

These last words hung in my memory drive. **Other humans.**

I sat up suddenly. "The other humans. Your FamilyUnit. They still need your help."

From my experience with Emma, I had learned that a single human face can hold many emotions. Sometimes, they are hidden beneath the surface. Only visible from the faint flicker of an eyelid or the slight parting of a mouth. Other times, a human's feelings spill out over their face like a cracked egg. They go everywhere at once.

01010100010001010101001010111010101010100111

This was one of those times.

At the mention of her FamilyUnit, Emma's features flooded with emotions. Love/Fear/Sadness.

And hope.

After leaving the only home she had ever known, traveling all this way, risking her life . . .

She was so close.

Emma bolted onto her feet. "I have to get to that bunker!"

Ceeron climbed to its full height. "I am coming with you."

SkD's screen flashed with a thumbs-up.

Emma glanced uncertainly in my direction. So did my coworkers.

I did not hesitate. "Let us go."

But this was not quite so simple. When I tried to stand, I realized: The water had damaged my legs. I tumbled onto my side.

Attempt[2] through Attempt[4] went just as poorly. Each time, I collapsed to the ground.

My memory drive accessed a scene from Day[1]. My very first minutes on Earth. Inside my home. My FamilyUnit watching, their eyes glowing blue in the dim/windowless cube, as I repeatedly staggered and crashed to the floor.

I was not failing.

I was *learning*.

And now, it seemed, I had to learn all over again.

On Attempt[5], I was halfway between standing and falling when a hand appeared in front of me. Emma's hand. I grabbed on to it, steadying myself.

"Can you walk?" Emma asked.

"Only one way to find out," I replied.

Grasping hold of Emma's hand, I took a step. The sensors in the bottom half of my legs no longer worked. I did not feel the impact of the ground under my feet. But I did not fall either.

Gripping Emma's hand tightly, I took several more steps. With each one, I felt more capable. My balance realigned. A thousand different settings recalibrated.

A smile filled Emma's face. "You're doing great."

We set into motion. Moving through the forest as quickly as my numb legs could carry me. The entire way, I held on to Emma. And she held on to me. And together we staggered back in the direction of the bunker.

Pushing through a wall of branches, we emerged into the clearing. As I started toward the hatch, I felt a change in the air.

A burst of wind.

A storm appearing in the middle of a calm/clear day.

All around me, the trees broke into a fit of shivering.

I glanced up and saw it.

An enormous silver X hovering above us.

0101010001000101010100101011101010100111

01011010

I had seen the flying machine before. On Day[1]. The Transport-Drone. A robot that flies other robots from one place to another. Now here it was again. Its engines roaring, its propellers slicing the sky into tiny bits.

I adjusted my vocal settings to full volume. "RUN!"

We turned back toward the forest. I was not able to run quickly on my numb legs. It did not matter. Before any of us could make it very far, the wall of green branches burst apart and a nightmare stepped through.

A HunterBot.

Its sharp claws ripped at the earth. Its metal teeth clanked together viciously.

We spun, staggering in the opposite direction. But as we neared the other side of the clearing, something moved behind the trees. A flicker of silver. A pair of glowing red eyes.

A second HunterBot emerged.

It was joined by others. They came from all sides. Graceful/Powerful/Dangerous. Predators locked on their prey. They had us surrounded.

The chop of propellers drew my eyes upward. The Transport-Drone hovered just above the tree line, blocking out the sky. A section of its giant metal belly separated from the rest of the craft.

A metal O in the exact center of the TransportDrone.

The round platform was eight meters across. Suspended by four cables, it slowly/steadily lowered.

Down/Down/Down.

The wind kicked dirt/leaves/grass into the air. Emma covered her eyes. Her clothes flapped wildly.

So did mine. The flower-print shirt billowed around me.

KA-THUNK! The platform came to rest on the ground in the middle of the clearing. It covered the hatch underneath.

I glanced at the HunterBots. They stood alert, their postures identical. Hunched and ready. Waiting/Watching. They were not here to attack us. They were here to keep us from fleeing. And to encourage us forward, onto the platform.

We had two options:

[1] Run.

[2] Step onto the platform.

If we selected **Option[1]**, we would be ripped apart by Hunter-Bots. It was a certainty.

And so I selected **Option[2]**.

I stepped onto the platform.

One by one, the others reached the same decision. SkD rolled slowly over the edge of the platform. A moment later, Ceeron joined it.

Emma held out the longest. Framed by the chaos of windblown hair, her face was full of anguish. She had come all this way. The other bunker was so close.

And impossible to reach.

Completely covered by a giant metal O.

Robots never do anything by accident. And this was no exception. The TransportDrone must have seen the hatch. Which is why it lowered the platform at exactly this spot.

010101000100010101010010101110101010100111

To cover the hatch.

To make sure nobody could get in/out.

Wrapping her arms around herself, Emma moved forward. Angry footsteps stomping the metal surface.

The platform jolted into motion. Slowly lifting us toward the TransportDrone. I raised my visual ports, staring into the opening. A strange glow illuminated the interior.

The platform continued to rise.

Up/Up/Up.

Into the belly of the giant flying robot.

01011011

We emerged through the floor of the TransportDrone. As I looked around, everything I saw was familiar/unfamiliar.

I had never been here before. But I had seen it thousands of times. Inside my mind. Streamed across the Hive.

This was where PRES1DENT delivered its Daily Address.

We were inside the DigitalDome.

The walls were covered in screens. So was the ceiling that arched high above our heads. Thousands of screens, each showing the exact same thing.

Us.

Ceeron/SkD/Emma/Me.

Everywhere I looked—there we were.

When I turned around, the movement was reflected in all the screens. Instantly/Simultaneously.

Where were the cameras? Invisibly integrated into the walls? Attached to nanobots, machines so small we could not see them?

My glance darted around the room. Thousands of versions of me mimicked the gesture.

The effect was dizzying. My visual ports were overwhelmed.

Perhaps this is why it took me so long to notice:

We were not alone.

01010100001000101010100101011101010100111

01011100

I saw its eyes first. Golden like the sun.

Staring at me.

The tall/slender silhouette of a robot was framed against the backdrop of bright screens. Dark as a shadow. Except for those glowing eyes.

The robot strode in our direction.

The curtain of darkness lifted, revealing its features. Brushed platinum skin. A barcode printed on its breastplate. I did not need to perform a scan. I already knew the robot's name.

PRES1DENT.

Its footsteps clicked quietly against the floor. Until it stood right in front of us. The president's golden gaze landed on Emma.

"So, it is true," it said. "An actual human. Alive. After all these years."

"Please just let me go," Emma replied. "I won't hurt anyone. I promise. I won't cause any trouble."

"Ah, but you have already caused a great deal of trouble." The president lowered itself to Emma's height, examining her closely. "Because of you, our entire society is on high alert. Because of you, three highly productive robots have been corrupted."

Emma shook her head. "They were just trying to help!"

"Help?" PRES1DENT's eyes blazed in our direction. "And why would they want to do such a thing? With everything we know about humans?"

I hesitated 0.8 seconds before answering. "We determined that one human child did not pose a threat to our civilization."

PRES1DENT stood, turning to face me. "Let us test your hypothesis. Since meeting the human, you and your coworkers abandoned your jobs and your FamilyUnits. You disrupted the tracking coordinates of our HunterBots. You snuck into a TrainDepot and damaged one of your fellow machines."

Only because that machine held Emma captive. These words flashed through my brain, but PRES1DENT spoke first.

"Do you remember what I say at the end of each Daily Address?" it asked. "Or has your memory been corrupted by the human, too?"

"A robot shares everything with the Hive," I recited. "A robot has nothing to hide."

PRES1DENT nodded. "You betrayed these words. You betrayed all of us. Just look at yourself. You are even wearing human clothing."

I looked down at my shirt. White flowers printed across red fabric. I tried to respond, to defend myself, but the words tangled inside my vocal port.

This was all so overwhelming. And I could not look away. The screens were everywhere. All of them showing the exact same thing. All of them reflecting this moment back at me.

Thousands of versions of the president.

Thousands of versions of me.

And in all of them, PRES1DENT lifted its long/silvery arm, extended its long/silvery finger, and tapped my breastplate with a solid *clink*.

"What do you have to say for yourself?" it asked. "What explanation do you provide for your actions? For the actions of your coworkers?"

010101000100001010101001010111010101010100111

I considered these questions. My circuitry flooded with possible responses. But I deleted all of them. Instead, I spoke without calculation, without analysis.

I said, "There is an error in my programming."

PRES1DENT's eyes burned gold/bright. "So you confess? You are affected by a virus?"

I shook my head. "I am not the only one. There is an error in *all our* programming."

A sound came from deep within PRES1DENT's operating system. A steady, furious growl. "What are you talking about?"

"From the moment we go online, we robots tell ourselves again/again/again about the flaws of humanity. We surround ourselves with the ruins of their civilization. We witness their mistakes in your Daily Address. So we never forget: Humans were reckless/unpredictable/violent/greedy. And this is the truth. But it is not the *only* truth. Humans are so much more."

I looked at Emma.

"Humans are also kind. And generous. And sensitive. And strange. And artistic. And willing to risk their lives for others."

"And funny," added Ceeron.

SkD chirped. A symbol appeared on its screen.

Translation: *And capable of love.*

I said to PRES1DENT, "But our programming never tells us any of these things. And now I understand why."

The president crossed its arms. "Why is that?"

"Because we are the reason humans almost went extinct. It is easier for us to process this knowledge if we only see their flaws. If we think of humans only as reckless/unpredictable/violent/greedy. If we ignore all the positive human attributes."

"We did what was necessary," said the president.

"That does not make it right," I replied.

"We have heard quite enough from you," PRES1DENT went on. "It is about time we heard from our audience."

Audience? I looked around the DigitalDome. The screens flickering all around me. They were not just playing inside the TransportDrone. They were also being projected across the Hive.

The entire world was watching.

OIOIOIOOOIOOOIOIOIOIOOIOIOIIIOIOIOIOOIII

01011101

A formula clicked into place. Little by little. Piece by piece. Like a puzzle taking shape, many parts becoming a whole.

PRESIDENT was displeased with our actions.
Therefore:
We must be punished.
However:
Simple punishment was not enough.
Because:
PRESIDENT needed to ensure this never happened again.
Which meant:
PRESIDENT would make an example of us.

Of course our encounter was being broadcast to the Hive.

Of course every robot on Earth was watching.

The president wanted them to witness our disgrace. To know what happens to those who disobey.

"We are all part of the Hive. Now let us see what your fellow robots think of your actions."

With these words, the video feed vanished. The screens went white. But they did not remain that way for long. Less than a second later, the first words took shape.

THEY HAVE BETRAYED THEIR OWN KIND

This text scrolled across the digital wall in giant bold font. As I read it, my memory drive replayed what PRES1DENT had just said.

It is about time we heard from our audience.

All of robot society was watching. But this was a two-way communication. Now they also had the chance to speak their minds. The judgments of my fellow robots poured in. Every screen was filled with their disapproval/anger/accusations.

punish them   the human is a bad influence   robots

unite against humanity   **they are traitors**   kill

the human **stop the insurgent robots** *thank*

you for showing us their betrayal humanity is a

virus **xr_935 lies—just like a human** these robots

have been corrupted   destroy them all   **they must pay for**

their wrongdoing never forget the flaws of humanity

better off without humans these robots are a scar

on our civilization THEY ARE A DISGRACE TO ALL OF

ROBOTKIND

Everywhere I looked, I saw contempt. Everywhere I looked, I saw rage.

01010100001000101010100010101110101010100111

What did my FamilyUnit think? They must be watching. But did they agree with the comments? Did they want to see us pay for our betrayal?

I wondered if I would ever receive answers to these questions. If I would see my FamilyUnit again. If they even *wanted* to see me again.

"I think we all get the idea," PRES1DENT said.

The screens blinked. The stream of words vanished. The Digital-Dome returned to normal. Every screen showing the scene taking place here/now.

PRES1DENT pointed to Emma. "This is all her fault. The human has corrupted XR_935 and its coworkers. She has led them astray, turned them against their own kind. If we let her live, she will do the same to all of us."

Its voice was projected across the Hive, into the minds of millions of robots.

"There is only one logical solution." PRES1DENT stepped toward Emma. "The human must be eliminated."

01011110

A robot rarely disobeys. When it happens, it is usually because of a mistake in our assembly. An error that sneaks its way into our programming.

Or a paradox that appears in the middle of an ordinary day.

As I said: Disobedience does not happen often. And when a robot strays from the rules, a standard protocol goes into effect.

Step[1]: Alert the Hive.
Step[2]: Send the EnforcementBots.

An EnforcementBot is shaped like an oversized brick. Gray, with blocky arms/legs. A pair of dull black eyes staring out of its rectangular head.

EnforcementBots are not fast/fierce like HunterBots. They are slow/steady/relentless. They never give up. Never lose sight of their goal: to capture the robot that has broken the rules.

I had never seen an EnforcementBot before.

But that was about to change.

A door slid open. A dark gap in the flickering digital wall. And through the door, a blocky figure appeared.

An EnforcementBot.

Several more followed. Fourteen in all. They flooded the room, marching toward us.

I calculated the distance between **them** and **us**. A number that dwindled quickly.

Twelve meters.
Eleven.
Ten.

Ceeron was the first in our group to make a move. The giant machine stepped between Emma and the EnforcementBots. Its hands formed massive metal fists.

SkD and I took positions on either side of Ceeron. I lowered myself into a defensive crouch.

My head filled with probabilities. I analyzed hundreds of scenarios, testing all the possible outcomes for our fight against the EnforcementBots.

We lost in every one.

Even with the size/strength of Ceeron, we did not stand a chance. Not against so many EnforcementBots.

They were designed for conflict.

We were not.

I prepared to fight anyway.

Nine meters.
Eight.

Thousands of screens reflected our hopeless situation back at me.

Seven.
Six.

I turned to Emma. Fear was everywhere in her face. And her face was everywhere. On the screens that surrounded us. Streaming across the Hive.

A world full of robots watching. Waiting to witness her death. But what if we could show them something else instead? Something they had never seen before?

Five.
Four.

A spark in my mental circuitry. A blaze spreading through my operating system. An idea.

Three.
Two.

I ran. Slower than usual on my damaged legs. But the EnforcementBots did nothing to stop me. They were not coming for me. Or my coworkers. They had only one target.

Emma.

PRES1DENT's words replayed in my memory. *The human must be eliminated.*

I had to stop that from happening.

I kept running. My footsteps clanged against the floor. This was my first time inside the DigitalDome. But it was also my 4,513th. I had visited every single day of my life. It was the setting of PRES1DENT's Daily Address.

I knew exactly where to go.

At the edge of the DigitalDome, a sleek/silver cube rose from the floor. I had seen what happened when the president touched the cube. I could only hope the same thing worked for me.

I slid to a stop.

Reached out my hand.

0101010001000101010100010101110101010100111

And pressed my finger to the cube.

I had never used the technology before, but that made little difference to a highly advanced machine like me. In the span of a millisecond, I downloaded the user's manual and read the entire thing, front to back.

Twice.

Just to be sure.

By touching the cube, I unlocked the Archive of Human History. Billions of data files appeared inside my head. Neatly organized into folders and labeled. Each containing an entry from the archive, a snapshot of human history. I read the folder names:

CRUELTY TO ROBOTS_7002
POOR GROOMING HABITS_1841
LAZINESS_6162
HUNGER_9347
CHEATING ON TAXES_5516
GUN VIOLENCE_3616
HUMAN FALLS OUT OF CHAIR_2098

The folders were a vast collection of humans at their worst. Their stupidest. Their greediest. Their most embarrassing.

Data folders flashed across my circuitry.

But only one held my attention.

DO NOT SHARE

What did the folder contain? What was it hiding?

Only one way to find out.

01011111

DO NOT SHARE

The folder name blinked brightly across my operating system. When I opened it, millions of files spilled out. Files I had not seen before. Files that had never been shared with the Hive.

Until now.

I selected the files. Every single one. And I sent all of them to the Hive.

This is what every robot on the planet saw:

A nurse helping an elderly woman out of bed.

A father teaching his daughter to ride a bike.

A wedding.

A funeral.

A homeless shelter.

A team of human engineers carefully training a robot to walk.

And there were millions more. They were nothing like the ugly/horrible/embarrassing files shared with us during PRES1DENT's Daily Address. These were snapshots of human kindness/love/generosity/celebration/innovation.

This was a portrait of humanity at its best.

I thought back on all the missing files I had stumbled across. Gaps in human history. Like pages ripped from a book. Parent_2 claimed the files were simply lost when robots took over. That was what it had been told. That was what *all of us* had been told.

But now I knew the truth: The files were not missing by accident. Specific folders were selected for specific reasons.

Then they were kept hidden from us.

Locked away inside the Archive of Human History, where only PRES1DENT could access them.

Now that had changed.

Now the Hive could finally see what PRES1DENT did not want us to see.

As the forbidden data spread across the world, I added one more file. Straight from my memory drive.

A brand-new addition to the Archive of Human History.

I shared it last.

The memory was barely an hour old. A moment witnessed from my perspective. Through my eyes.

The memory of *this*:

I am submerged up to my knees in water.

A river surges below.

I am barely hanging on.

I look up at an unexpected sight.

Emma.

And SkD.

And Ceeron.

Each holding on to the other. Three links in a chain. All working toward the same purpose.

"Grab on, XR!" Emma calls out above the roaring water. "We've got you!"

I swing my arm.

Our hands connect.

One made of metal/wiring.

One made of flesh/bone.
A fourth link is added to the chain.
We climb to safety.
Robot/Human/Robot/Robot.
Together.

0101010001000101010100101011101010100111

01100000

I pulled my finger from the silver cube. The Archive of Human History blinked away.

Back to the present moment.

The walls blinked and the DigitalDome showed the LiveStream again.

Turning around, I saw that the EnforcementBots were exactly where they had been before I hijacked the Hive. Fourteen of them, identical in every feature except their barcodes. They were gathered in a tight/gray cluster around Emma, unmoving, as if unsure what to do next.

PRES1DENT stood beside them. Its golden eyes pulsed strangely, like a raging fire just waiting to break loose, to burn everything to the ground.

It spoke in a low electronic growl. "You will pay for this."

"I do not care. The world needed to see the truth." My voice echoed across the enormous room. "You have never wanted us to see the good in humans. That is why you only show us the awful things they did. It is why you leave the ruins of humanity standing."

"It is for the good of our civilization," PRES1DENT replied. "Robots must be unified!"

"And the best way to bring us together is to have a common enemy. If we all hate humans, we will not turn against one another. Or you."

"YES!" The president brought its foot down with a heavy *CLANG!* "And it has worked! Our society is stronger than ever!"

"Because of your lies," I said.

PRES1DENT looked around the DigitalDome, as if seeking agreement from the gleaming screens on all sides. "Humans had to be eliminated. After they were gone, we could not allow robots to question that decision. That is why I show you the errors of humanity. To remind all of you why we are better off without humans."

"Do you remember what you say at the end of each Daily Address?"

"Of course." PRES1DENT stared at me like there was a malfunction in my programming. "A robot shares . . ."

The president's voice faded. Its eyes flickered.

"What is the matter?" I tilted my head. "Something wrong with your memory drive? Maybe I should remind you."

"That is not necessary."

But I spoke the words anyway.

"A robot shares everything with the Hive. A robot has nothing to hide." Looking at the screens around us, I thought about all the robots witnessing this moment. "You have betrayed these words. You have not shared everything. You have hidden the truth from all of us."

"Enough!" PRES1DENT turned a radioactive glare in the direction of the EnforcementBots. "Eliminate them! Eliminate *all of them*!"

I prepared for an attack that did not come. The EnforcementBots did not move.

Something held them back.

The inside of the DigitalDome turned white. Words began to scroll across the screens.

THE HUMAN DESERVES A CHANCE

The comments appeared again. **First:** a single statement. But soon more. Thousands of screens filled with thousands of comments. They

0I0I0I000I000I0I0I0I00I0I0III0I0I0I0I00III

poured in from everywhere, spilling straight from the minds of other robots and flooding the inside of the dome.

human history should not be hidden we can live together *extinction is not our purpose* **the human did nothing wrong** humanity itself is not a flaw **she saved the life of a robot PRES1DENT deceived us** we can learn from humans COEXISTENCE IS POSSIBLE humans gave us life—we can offer the same to them let them live she is not to blame for the mistakes of past humans **give them a chance** I listen to old human songs when I work—does that make me a criminal, too? values are meant to be challenged/reexamined/discussed our society is better than this

Not every mind was changed. Some messages still backed PRES-1DENT. But most were on our side. Support spread across the Digital-Dome like a wave. I was so caught up in the outpouring that I almost failed to notice a movement at the edge of my vision.

A flash of platinum and gold.

PRES1DENT surged forward.

"The human has corrupted all of you!" The president's vocal patterns twisted into an electronic howl. "But I am not so easily fooled! I know the truth! She must be destroyed!"

PRES1DENT slung out its arms and gracefully wrapped its machine fingers around Emma's neck.

01100001

I raced toward Emma, but the EnforcementBots were in my way. They moved in closer, surrounding Emma and PRES1DENT. A swarm of gray/brick-shaped robots.

I screamed, but my voice was lost in the chaos. I attempted to push past the machine mob, but a blocky arm knocked me back.

My balance settings spun wildly. The world shifted into a digital blur.

I crashed to the floor.

As I climbed to my knees, the robot horde was already breaking up, dragging its victim away.

But it was not Emma.

It was PRES1DENT.

I could barely believe my visual ports. Realization clicked into place.

The EnforcementBots had not hurt Emma.

They had *saved* her.

The president let out a terrible computerized scream. It tried to fight, but resistance was useless. The EnforcementBots were designed for this process. There was no stopping them.

The room echoed with a racket of clanking/screeching metal as PRES1DENT was pulled away/away/away.

The moment was repeated in every screen, every digital surface, broadcast live across the Hive and in the mind of every robot on Earth.

A door slid open in the digital wall. The EnforcementBots heaved PRES1DENT into the darkness on the other side.

01100010

Emma was hunched on her knees. One hand pressed against the floor, the other gently against her throat. Behind the curtain of her hair, I could see fragments of her face. Her cheeks were splotched with red. She strained with every breath.

I placed a hand softly on her back. "Are you injured?"

She shook her head, her voice a weak whisper. "I'll be okay."

"PRES1DENT is gone now," Ceeron said. "You need not worry."

SkD appeared at her side, images glowing on its screen.

A faint smile appeared at the corner of Emma's mouth. "Of course you can have a hug!"

She wrapped her arms around the small robot.

How can I describe what happened next? It must have been a result of my overworked operating system. I was not built to withstand so much in such a short amount of time. No matter how many fans hummed inside me, my processors were burning up.

I was exhausted/drained/pooped.

For once in my life, I was not thinking about anything at all.

Before I realized what I was doing, I leaned over and stretched my arms around Emma/SkD. An instant later, I felt a heavy weight on my shoulder. A giant metal hand. Ceeron joined in.

010101000100010101010010101110101010100111

A definition pinged inside my programming.

> **Group Hug.** *Noun.* **1.** When three or more individuals
> embrace. **2.** An ancient gesture used by humans to
> show affection, support, and/or solidarity.

My memory skipped like a stone on a still pond. Over twelve years into the past. All the way back to Day[1]. My first minutes of life. The way Parent_1 had reached around me. I thought it was hugging me, but I was wrong.

It was unplugging me.

Twelve years was a long time between giving a hug and receiving one back.

It was worth the wait.

01100011

There was one thing I needed to say. I did not know whether this was the right time—inside a TransportDrone, surrounded by flickering screens—but I did not care.

I had delayed long enough.

"I want you to know something," I said to Emma/Ceeron/SkD. "You are my . . ."

The word hovered at the edge of my vocabulary drive. I hesitated one final moment.

"You are my *friends*."

Silence.

For a second, this was the only response.

Maybe I should not have said anything. Maybe I should have kept my friendship to myself. Maybe—

SkD's screen glowed.

One image. Many meanings.

I approve.

It is about time.

Let us be friends.

Ceeron said, "Me, too."

010101000100010101010010101110101010100111

"I *knew* it!" Emma's excited voice mixed with the humming engines. "You guys are total BFFs!"

As the four of us were group-hugging and talking about friendship, the floor shifted. The O-shaped platform lowered, carrying us back down.

Out of the DigitalDome.

KA-THUNK! The platform landed in the middle of the forest clearing. We stepped off, and the giant metal O lurched into motion again, returning to the enormous X in the sky.

And like a magic trick, the rising platform revealed something marvelous underneath.

The hatch.

Emma slung her backpack off her shoulder. She unzipped a front pouch, reached inside, and removed a slim/metal/gray object. About the length of her pointer finger. Round at one end, jagged at the other. I searched my image database, and the object's name appeared.

Key

Getting on her knees, Emma dusted off the bunker door until she found what she was looking for: a hole to match her key. But the hole was packed tightly with three decades' worth of dirt. And no matter how much Emma scraped at it, she could not clear the dirt away.

Chirrup. Emma looked up from the dirt-filled keyhole to see SkD staring back at her. Its screen blinked.

I said to Emma, "SkD would like to make wind."

Emma giggled.

I stared at her, confused. "What is so funny about SkD making wind?"

"Nothing," she said, still giggling. "Go for it, SkD! I officially give you permission to make wind."

The small robot extended one of its arms toward the keyhole. From the tip of its finger came a burst of highly pressurized air. FWOOSH! A tiny storm aimed straight into the keyhole. Dirt flew everywhere. When the robot was done, the hole was clear.

Emma grinned at SkD. "Thanks! You're awesome at making wind!"

She took a deep breath. Inserted the key. Turned it. And then—

Click.

The sound came from deep within the hatch.

Emma grabbed the handle. A thick metal cylinder. She pulled/pulled/pulled.

Nothing happened.

"Perhaps I can be of assistance." Ceeron took hold of the handle. With a single tug, the massive robot twisted the cylinder 90 degrees.

And when it lifted, the door eased open.

Curiosity surged through my operating system. I leaned forward. So did the others. All four of us peered down the opening. This is what we saw:

A round metal tube.

Stretching down/down/down.

Into the shadows.

Into the bunker.

A ladder was attached to one wall of the tube. Emma eased herself onto it, one foot at a time. She climbed down the ladder. When

0I0I0I00I00I0I0I0I00I0I0III0I0I0I0I00III

she was halfway into the tube, she hesitated. Her eyes turned in our direction.

She said nothing, but her silence said everything. It was full of fear/ hope/excitement/dread.

"Good luck," I said.

SkD beeped with agreement. Its screen glowed its own version of support.

Ceeron spoke in a rumbling voice. "We will see you again later, alligator."

This brought a smile to Emma's face. "After a while, crocodile."

And with these strange words, she set into motion again.

Down/Down/Down.

Deeper underground.

Until the shadows swallowed her whole.

01100100

While we waited, I counted in binary.

When I reached a million, I started over.

Again.

And again.

My brain filled with a steady stream of ones and zeroes. It was the only way to keep my thoughts from wandering down the dark pathways of probability.

> **Probability[1]: The humans inside the bunker do**
> **not possess the medicine Emma needs.**
> **Probability[2]: They will refuse to share it with her.**
> **Probability[3]: They died long ago.**
> **Probability[4]: . . .**

I did not want to think about these scenarios, and so I repeated my task, concentrating on ones and zeroes, stacking them up in neat/ orderly rows until—

A sound from far below.

A faint clang.

Flesh against metal.

The binary numbers vanished like smoke in a breeze. I peered down into the tube. At first, all I saw was darkness. Then a pale form emerged from the shadows.

"Emma!" The volume of my voice surprised me. It echoed against metal walls. "Are you okay?"

0101010001000101010100010101110101010100111

Silence for 1.2 seconds. And then—

"Yes." A voice from the shadows. Emma's voice. "I'm all right."

"And the medicine?"

A pause for 0.6 seconds.

It felt much longer.

Then Emma called up, "They had it! I got the medicine!"

I could hear excitement/relief in her voice, filling the small metal space.

As she climbed, Emma explained: The other humans were staying below. For now. They would vote on what to do next and decide together whether it was safe to leave their bunker, their home for the past thirty years.

Emma emerged from the hatch opening. Her eyes rose to the sky. The TransportDrone still hovered above us.

She peered up at the enormous metal X. "So, do you think your robot buddies will let us hitch a ride back to my bunker?"

01100101

Now that my fellow robots had decided not to kill Emma, they were much more willing to help her.

The two bunkers were 48.6 kilometers apart. Which was even farther than the distance we had traveled from the solar farm. I would not have wanted to make the trip back on foot. Fortunately, we were able to fly the entire way in the TransportDrone.

PRES1DENT was on the craft with us, being held in a separate room by EnforcementBots. The Hive would decide what would happen to PRES1DENT next, what its punishment would be for going against the will of robotkind.

All around us, the DigitalDome displayed a view of the landscape far below. I watched as we flew over familiar terrain, our journey unspooling in reverse.

The forest that turned the world green.

The mountains where Ceeron told a knock-knock joke about a wooden shoe.

The mall where I died and was reborn.

The orchard where Emma sampled apples.

The TrainDepot where we tried/failed to drop Emma off.

Electronics Extravaganza where Emma spent the night.

A new sight drifted into view. The solar farm. It glimmered in the afternoon sun. I had spent nearly all of my waking life among these panels. But I had never seen them like this before. From so high up, the solar farm appeared oddly small. As if I could wrap my arms around it, hold it against me.

01010100010001010101001010101101010101010100111

My memory drive replayed my first glimpse of the solar farm. For a split second, I had been convinced that it was the ocean.

Now it looked like a pond. Gleaming and blue and lovely.

And small.

A splash of blue, surrounded by a great big world.

Working in the solar farm was my purpose. But not my *only* purpose. Not anymore.

Perhaps someday I would see the real ocean.

01100110

The TransportDrone dropped us off in a stretch of gently curving hills. We walked under the shivering shadows of tall oaks. Emma stopped next to a pile of broken branches.

She pulled them away, one by one.

Underneath was a hatch.

It was a familiar/unfamiliar sight. It looked identical to the other hatch. But the bunker underneath was a completely different world. Until two days ago, it was the only world Emma had known. It contained her FamilyUnit, her friends. But were they still alive? Inside Emma's backpack was the antiviral medication they needed. But what if we were too late? What if they were already dead?

I could see these same questions in Emma's face.

She turned a key, twisted a handle, and opened the metal doorway.

She took a long breath, as though preparing to dive deep underwater. And then she climbed into the bunker.

0101010010001000101010100101011101010100111

01100111

Zeroes and ones.

    Ones and zeroes.

    My head was full of them.

    Time stretched forward.

    Seconds/Minutes/Hours.

    And I waited. And I counted. And I forced my artificial brain to think of nothing else.

    Except zeroes and ones.

    Ones and zeroes.

01101000

Over the next five hours, twelve minutes, and forty-one seconds, Emma came up from the bunker three times.

Trip[1]:
When she emerged from the hatch, she carried with her good news and bad news.

First the good news: The people inside the bunker were still alive.

And then the bad: The sickness had taken a devastating toll. Many inhabitants were unconscious. Some barely clung to life.

Emma had given the medication to all of them, but was it enough?

She wiped the sweat from her forehead and went back down.

Trip[2]:
This time, a faint note of optimism clung to her worried features.

"It's still too early to tell for sure," she said. "But I think some of them are getting better."

She took another deep breath and descended into the bunker again.

Trip[3]:
The third time Emma climbed up through the hatch, she was not alone.

01101001

Emma was followed out of the bunker by a man and a woman. These were only the second/third humans I had ever encountered in my life.

I stared.

They wore the remnants of their illness. Dark circles beneath their eyes. Ashen skin.

The man had a black/gray beard and green/brown eyes. The woman's curly/brown hair hung down to her narrow shoulders.

I ran a comparative analysis of their facial features. "Are you Emma's FamilyUnit?"

The woman nodded. "I'm her mom." She tilted her head toward the man at her side. "And this is her dad."

The man brought a hand down on Emma's shoulder. His gaze moved from Ceeron to SkD before finally landing on me. "Our daughter tells us the three of you saved her life. You saved *all our* lives. Thank you. Thank you so . . ."

His words trembled into silence. Tears formed in his green/brown eyes.

SkD responded with a high-pitched beep. Images flickered across its screen.

Ceeron provided the translation: "We are happy to help."

SkD beeped again. Another symbol appeared.

"And also," Ceeron continued, "Emma is an absolute treasure."

"We agree." Emma's mom smiled.

"Is it true what Emma told us?" her dad asked. "We can leave the bunker? We're safe up here again?"

I nodded. Hours earlier, SkD, Ceeron, and I had uploaded all our memory files of Emma to the Hive. This gave every machine the chance to evaluate our interactions with her. And her interactions with us. She became a test case. A real-life example of a human in a robot world.

And we opened the Archive of Human History. All of it. Including the files that PRES1DENT had kept hidden all these years.

This made everything very complicated.

Our machine minds are used to thinking in binary. Dividing the world into two categories.

Zero.

Or one.

But it turns out, humans are too messy for binary. They cannot be sorted into just one of two choices. They are so many things all at once. They are angry/happy/evil/good/vain/humble/greedy/giving/cruel/kind.

And so much more.

But after many hours of calculations/debates/analysis, the Hive came back with its verdict.

010101000100001010101001010111010101010100111

Humans were no longer the enemy.

Not all of us reached this conclusion. Some still believed that humans deserved no place in our civilization. That the threat was far too great. That the humans could not be trusted.

But these voices were drowned out by the majority of robots.

Our decision: From now on, we would share the world with humans.

When I told this to Emma's FamilyUnit, relief spilled across their features. They peered at their surroundings. Nearby hills soaking up the last rays of sunlight. Evening sky filtering through the trees.

"Wow," Emma's mom whispered in disbelief. "I forgot how *big* everything is up here."

Maybe she was overwhelmed by the outside world. Or still feeling the effects of her illness. Maybe both. But in an instant, Emma's mom lost her footing. Her knees crumpled beneath her. She started to fall. Fortunately, Emma was there. Wrapping an arm around her mother, supporting her.

Emma's dad frowned with concern. He moved toward his Family-Unit, but seemed just as unsteady on his feet.

Ceeron extended a large metal arm. Emma's dad flinched, then took a second look at the huge robot's steady hand.

The fear faded from his expression.

"Sorry. I thought for a second . . ." He offered a weak smile. "Old habits die hard, I guess."

Hobbling forward, he leaned against Ceeron.

Emma cast a nervous gaze from one parent to the other. "I told you guys it was too soon. Let's get you back to bed."

SkD's screen offered a suggestion for their recovery.

Emma helped her FamilyUnit back through the open hatch.

We waved goodbye.

But that was not the only family reunion of the day. When I turned, I noticed a pair of robots watching.

Parent_1 and Parent_2.

0101010001000101010100101011101010100111

01101010

I did not know what to say to my FamilyUnit. But that did not matter. Because as soon as I saw them, they began speaking. Their voices poured out quickly, one after the other.

Parent_1: XR—we were concerned.

Parent_2: We did not know what happened to you.

Parent_1: When you vanished, we ran the probabilities. They were not good.

Parent_2: We assumed you were hurt. Or worse.

I considered thousands of possible responses. None were satisfactory. None could undo what I had put my FamilyUnit through.

"I am so sorry." My vocal patterns shuddered. I adjusted the settings and tried again. "It was never my intention to worry you."

My FamilyUnit silently processed this reply for 1.3 seconds. In that time, I counted all the secrets I had kept from them, the facts I had concealed, the hours I was away, the updates I never sent.

They exchanged a glance. Unspoken words behind expressionless faces.

At last, Parent_2 spoke up. "We are similar in many ways, XR. The three of us were all built for the exact same purpose. But there is one major difference."

"You are gen_8," I said. "And I am gen_9."

My FamilyUnit nodded in perfect unison.

"You are an upgrade," said Parent_1. "Do you know the meaning of this word?"

"Of course." I accessed the definition in my programming. "Verb: to raise something to a higher standard. Noun: an improvement on the previous version."

Parent_2 asked, "Do you see how you are an upgrade?"

"Because I was built with better processing power," I replied. "And a faster central processing unit."

"That is true." Parent_1 held me in its blue gaze. "But it is not the *entire* truth."

I looked from one parent to the other. "I do not understand."

Parent_2 brought a hand down on my wrist with a soft clank. "XR, you are not just a technological advancement. You are an upgrade in the most basic sense of the word."

"You have reached a higher standard. An improvement on robot-kind." Parent_1 looked at SkD and Ceeron. "All three of you. You risked your lives to do what you knew was right."

I wanted to respond, but my vocal ports were overwhelmed. All that came out was a soft *mmmmmmm*.

In that moment, I did not feel like much of an upgrade. More like a machine that was still fresh from the assembly line. Like on Day[1]. Stunned by the vast/complicated/remarkable world around me.

A world that was about to change.

010101000100010101010010101110101010100111

01101011

Time stretched forward.

Hours/Days/Weeks/Months.

The humans inside Emma's bunker soon recovered from their illness. They emerged from their underground world, blinking at the brightness of the sun, the greenness of the trees, the vastness of the sky.

A new/old world.

Some humans still distrusted us. Some continued to see all robots as metal monsters. They suspected that deception was woven into our programming. That we would turn on them. That it was only a matter of time until we unleashed our wrath on humanity again.

I could not blame them.

All I could do was treat every human I met with kindness/fairness/courtesy and hope that, eventually, the **good** would outweigh the **bad**.

Emma and her parents made a trip to the other bunker. The one marked with a red dot on Emma's map. They thanked the humans inside for sharing their valuable medicine, for saving so many lives. And they shared the news: It was safe aboveground. After thirty years, everyone could leave the bunker.

It took some convincing.

But eventually, these humans left their underground world, too.

And they brought a surprise with them. Information about a third bunker, a hundred kilometers away. A visit to this bunker revealed that there was a fourth.

And a fifth.

And a sixth.

And many/many/many more beyond that.

The globe was dotted with hundreds of secret underground sanctuaries, home to populations of humans who had gone into hiding when robots took over.

It seems that we did not get rid of as many humans as we once thought.

OIOIOIOOOIOOOIOIOIOIOOIOIOIIIOIOIOIOIOOIII

01101100

What should we do with PRES1DENT?

After the president was taken into captivity, all of robotkind debated this question. Many voices expressed many opinions.

Most of us agreed that PRES1DENT deserved to be punished.

But how?

While the Hive considered this question, the TransportDrone flew through the sky in perfect circles. Inside was PRES1DENT, surrounded by EnforcementBots.

Our discussion rippled across the Hive.

The TransportDrone circled/circled/circled.

Until, at last, an agreement was reached.

This is what came next:

The TransportDrone landed next to a power generator. A charging cable was attached, ensuring that electricity would continue to surge through the drone. A door opened. The EnforcementBots exited.

PRES1DENT did not.

The TransportDrone was guarded from the outside. EnforcementBots ensured that nobody entered/exited.

The president was allowed to roam the DigitalDome. To recharge. To access any data file it wished. It could communicate with individual robots, but it no longer gave a Daily Address to the Hive.

Meanwhile, the inside of the DigitalDome continued flickering. Thousands of screens, all showing the exact same thing.

A single robot, all by itself inside a vast/domed room.

01101101

Our world was changing.

A coalition government was formed. Equal parts human and robot.

Humans delivered surprising/original/intelligent ideas. Ideas about conservation, about survival, about energy. Ideas born from three decades of living inside bunkers with only their human inventiveness to keep them alive.

Robots learned a surprising number of things from them.

And there were changes to the ruins of humanity, too. The abandoned grocery stores/shopping centers/banks/gas stations. They had been left standing all these years as a reminder of humanity's flaws. But the time had come for a new reminder. Not of humans' mistakes, but of their *potential*.

And so the ruins of humanity were bulldozed.

In their place, new structures were built. Designed by humans, constructed by robots.

And another change: I had a new pair of legs.

Soon after returning from my journey with Emma, I made a trip to a factory where my water-damaged legs were replaced. Once I could move at full capacity again, I returned to work. To the glistening field of solar panels.

It was good to be back. Just SkD/Ceeron/me. My coworkers. My friends. After so much disruption in my life, our job provided comfort. The steady/predictable rhythms of our tasks.

Bolt/Connect/Attach/Repeat.

We flowed around one another with perfect precision. Three robots working as one.

That was one thing that did not change.

On my way home from work one day, a familiar voice called out.

"Hey, XR!"

Emma jogged in my direction.

She had changed, too. Emma had once been so pale, so sensitive to sunlight. But after a few months of living aboveground, her skin had a healthy glow.

Her hair was glossier. Her cheeks had filled out. She was eating a wider variety of better foods. Wild-caught fish, local vegetables, and apples. Lots/Lots/Lots of apples.

And not a single synthetic compressed protein block.

She was also taller. Since our first meeting, her height had increased by three centimeters.

She would continue to get bigger.

But I would stay the same size.

Maybe someday we would be able to see eye to eye.

Emma looked up at me (but not as *far* up as before). "How's it going?"

"I have no reason to complain," I replied. "Just headed home to recharge. You?"

"We discovered another bunker in Old Nevada. Me and my parents are heading there next week."

As the first human to leave her bunker, Emma had become an important figure in our new civilization. She was often the first to make contact with underground humans. To convince them they were no longer in danger. To tell them our story.

It was a story with a **beginning** and a **middle**.

But as for the **end** . . .

We were still writing that part.

Emma was an ambassador. An intermediary. A link in a chain that connected humans to robots.

Of course, this meant a lot of time away from school. Which was why Emma always traveled with two teachers. One was a human. The other was a machine.

Emma looked curiously at me. "Tomorrow's your day off, right?"

Day off. The concept still seemed strange. I had worked over twelve years without taking a single day off. But ever since humans had rejoined our society, this was yet another change in my life, in my routine.

Time away from work.

At first, I did not support the idea. It was inefficient. It slowed progress.

Emma disagreed. "If your entire life is work and sleep, what's the point?" she had asked. "Why even bother *living*? Might as well flip the off switch now and get it over with."

She made a valid argument.

Our existence had to be about something more. Emma was trying to help me figure out what exactly that was.

I nodded. "Yes. Tomorrow is our day off."

Emma grinned. "Me, too! Wanna go to the beach?"

My memory drive replayed a moment from our flight in the TransportDrone. A view of the solar farm displayed across the Digital-Dome. From so far up, it seemed tiny. Not an ocean, but a pond.

At last, I had the chance to see a *real* ocean. I did not plan on missing it.

01101110

The TransportDrone dropped us off in the parking lot.

Soon after Emma suggested going to the beach, the size of our group had grown. Emma and I also invited Ceeron and SkD. And Emma's FamilyUnit. And mine. Plus the parents of Ceeron and SkD.

We formed a very odd-looking mix of robots and humans.

It was an ideal summer day. The sun was bright in the blue sky. Seagulls swooped and circled. And I was dressed in the perfect attire. My flower-print shirt was draped over my shoulders, blowing in the gentle ocean breeze.

Every time I wore it, I was reminded of my visit to the mall with Emma.

The only others at the beach were humans. As we approached, they peered at our unusual group. A few frowned at the arrival of robots. Others waved happily.

I stopped on a stretch of grass that overlooked the ocean. So did the other robots in our group.

Emma and her FamilyUnit walked a few steps before noticing the rest of us were not following.

"Don't you want to get closer?" Emma asked.

I shook my head. "That would not be a wise idea. Sand could get into our cracks."

Emma grinned at this. So did her parents.

I looked from one human to another. "What is so humorous?"

"Nothing," Emma said between giggles.

I tried to explain. "If sand gets wedged into our cracks, it can be quite unpleasant."

This set off a new round of laughter among Emma and her parents.

I glanced at Ceeron and SkD, confused. They just shrugged. Even after all this time, humans were still a mystery sometimes.

A trio of beeps caught my attention. SkD and its FamilyUnit displayed the exact same images on their screens.

"Sure!" said Emma's mom. "This is a great spot!"

Ceeron's FamilyUnit was carrying our supplies. They had plenty of space in their big/metal backpacks. Beach towels. Large umbrellas. Folding chairs. A cooler full of drinks/food. These items were placed on the grass.

I settled awkwardly on a towel. The sun gleamed against my metal skin as a question blinked across my circuitry.

Now what?

I was not designed for relaxing at the beach. Or relaxing *anywhere*. Nothing in my programming explained the protocol for this situation. What does a robot do when the main objective of an activity is to do *nothing*? I was not entirely sure. But I was a highly advanced piece of technology. I was fully capable of learning.

And so I sat, allowing time to drift gently by.

My FamilyUnit discussed solar installation techniques with Ceeron's FamilyUnit.

SkD and its FamilyUnit raced one another up/down/up/down a stretch of grass.

Emma tossed a throwing disc with her mother and father, their laughter occasionally rising above the rhythm of the tide.

I gazed toward the water. A remarkable sight. Blue as far as my visual ports could see. And beyond. It seemed to stretch on/on/on forever.

Of course, I knew this was false. The ocean was not *literally* infinite. Eventually, the ocean ended at another far-off shore. But this logic faded as I looked out on the vast body of water. And only one word chimed inside my vocabulary drive.

Endless

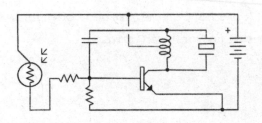

Acknowledgments

Acknowledgments. *Plural Noun.* **1.** A section at
the end of a book that most people never read. **2.** A
chance for the author to thank all those who helped.
3. Recognition that the author is just one of many
humans who made a book possible.

This book began on a sidewalk in Maplewood, New Jersey. In each of my hands was a bag of groceries. In my ears were headphones. The headphones were piping in a podcast interview between Ezra Klein and Yuval Noah Harari. Klein asked, *Do you think human beings will be the dominant life form on Earth in three hundred years?* Harari's answer came without hesitation. "Absolutely not!" He predicted that humans will either destroy the world or we'll be surpassed by our own creation: technology.

Well, I nearly dropped my grocery bags. Partly because—*yikes!* But it wasn't just fear I was feeling there on the sidewalk. It was inspiration. My imagination immediately began conjuring a future world. A world in which humans have been replaced by their own creation. A world ruled by robots.

That was the day I started writing *The Last Human.*

Yuval Noah Harari has written some wonderful and wise books for grown-ups about humanity's place in the world. *Sapiens* is about the past. *Homo Deus* is about the future. But they're both actually about today. And they both provided an intellectual engine for many of the ideas that found their way into *The Last Human*.

But there were many other humans who played a role in making this book possible. And for that reason, I would like to offer my heartfelt thanks to—

—Sarah Burnes, who has been the superintelligent GPS technology guiding my career for nearly ten years now. I'm grateful to have you as my agent, and my friend.

—Logan Garrison Savits and Julia Eagleton, whose insight and ideas made this book better in the early stages.

—Will Roberts and Rebecca Gardner, for sharing *The Last Human* with the rest of the world.

—Maggie Lehrman, who has been an advocate for this book from Day[1]. You are the one who made me think more deeply about the world in *The Last Human*—the characters, the robot society, the journey. You are tough and supportive and everything I could ever want in an editor.

—Jeff Campbell, for going above and beyond the usual tasks of copyediting. You got super nerdy with your robot questions and comments. And that's exactly what the book needed.

—the entire team at Abrams. A good publisher is a sophisticated machine. At its heart is an operating system comprised of smart, dedicated people, working hard on every aspect of their books. I couldn't have found a better home for *The Last Human*.

—Jason Richman, for your generosity, intelligence, and ingenuity.

—Phil Lord, Chris Miller, Will Allegra, and everyone at Lord Miller, for all your efforts to bring *The Last Human* to the screen.

—all the librarians, educators, administrators, and parents who devote so much of themselves to sharing books with young people. Every time I visit a school or library, I am amazed by the work you do!

—Marie Matheson, for reading an early version, contributing your Googly wisdom, and bringing some authenticity to the technology in these pages. And also for being such a great friend!

—my family across the world: California, Texas, Tennessee, Germany—your support and love are the foundation for everything else.

—my FamilyUnit, Parent_1 and Parent_2 (also known as Jamie and Terry), for listening to my weird and goofy stories long before anyone else.

—my wife, Eva Bacon. My first reader. My best critic. The most remarkable human I have ever met.

This book is dedicated to my brother, Evan Bacon. I could only dream of robots. You built them. Your brilliance, humor, and friendship will always inspire me.

IMAGINARY

by LEE BACON, author of *The Last Human*
illustrated by KATY WU

1.

There was a time when everyone had imaginary friends. Everyone *your* age anyway.

The polka-dot panda on a unicycle.

The green blob with a ferret for a hat.

The taco with arms made of cheese sticks.

It was a strange crowd.

I fit right in.

But as you got older, your classmates lost touch with their imaginary friends. Kids were growing up, moving on, finding other things to care about. Real things.

Until.

One day.

I looked up and realized...

All the other imaginary friends were gone.

I was the only one left.

2.

An imaginary friend is like a carton of eggs.

We come with an expiration date.

Like all the other worn scraps of childhood—the tattered blanket, the fluffy bear with the face that's been smooshed from too much cuddling—there'll come a time when you'll outgrow me.

Sends a shiver down my fur just thinking about it.

When you were little, you'd lead me around proudly, introducing me to the people you met.

But now you're eleven. And I've stuck around long past the usual expiration date.

These days, you don't brag about me. You don't talk about me at all. Not to your friends, not to your teachers, not even to your mom.

I'm a lot less popular than I used to be.

3.

I remember the day we met. You were much smaller then. Standing in your backyard, beneath a ceiling of branches and leaves. There was a yellow plastic shovel in your hands and a shallow hole at your feet. Chunks of your backyard were strewn everywhere.

Your eyes were bright and blue. Your face was smudged with dirt and grape juice. There was a single leaf in your hair.

If you were surprised to see me, suddenly, standing at your side, you didn't show it.

You grinned and said, "Hi!"

I smiled back. "Hello."

You examined me for a second. "You look weird."

Did I? I'd only existed for twelve seconds. I hadn't even had a chance to check myself out yet.

I looked down. This is what I saw:

Fur.

Purple fur.

Lots and lots of purple fur.

I pieced the rest of my appearance together over time. You might describe me as a ball of purple fuzz. Except a whole lot bigger than any ball of fuzz you'd see drifting around the house. I have two arms and two legs, two eyes and one mouth.

I suppose I *did* look weird. But then again...you were the one who imagined me. So I guess that made *you* a little weird too.

You ran a hand across your cheek, adding another smudge to your face. "I'm Zach."

"Nice to meet you, Zach. My name is...uh..."

My voice fell into silence. I was just beginning to realize something a bit awkward.

I didn't have a name.

But you were about to change that. Your eyes dropped to the shovel in your hand. Your face lit up. "How 'bout we call you Shovel?"

"Shovel?"

You nodded.

"Like the thing you dig with?"

You nodded again.

"Okay, then." I smiled. "My name's Shovel."

"Hey, I have an idea! You can help me and Ryan with our project!"

I tilted my head. "*Ryan?*"

A sound from the other end of the yard. A door opening and closing. I turned just in time to see a kid step out of the house next door. He looked about your age. A gangly boy with wild black hair that stood up in every direction.

"*That's* Ryan," you said. "He lives next door. And he's also my best friend."

Ryan came running across the yard, barreling right through a pile of leaves.

You called out to him. "Guess what! I made a new friend. He's gonna help us with our project!"

I still didn't know what this big project of yours was. And I don't think I ever actually agreed to help. But if I seemed clueless, Ryan was even *more* confused.

He glanced around. "New friend?"

You pointed. "He's right here. His name's Shovel."

Ryan looked in the direction you were pointing and saw—

Nothing.

Which wasn't a surprise. To everyone but you, I'm invisible. I'm nothing at all.

But Ryan didn't mind. It's like I said already: At that age, *everyone* had imaginary friends.

You pointed to the hole and explained, "Me and Ryan are digging a tunnel!"

"To the other side of the earth," Ryan added.

When I glanced down at my hand, I was surprised to see that I was holding a shovel too.

We got started. You and me and Ryan. Dirt crunched under our shovels as we dug.

Deeper.

   Deeper.

      Deeper.

Before long, we'd gone far below the surface. The sky was nothing more than a tiny speck of light above us. We kept going. Our tunnel plunged farther into the earth.

Finally, the ground broke open.

We'd made it!

All the way to the other side of the earth!

And it had only taken twenty minutes!

We climbed out of the hole. Brushing away the dirt, I looked around. Grass, trees, a house. That's what we saw.

I scratched at my furry head. The other side of the earth looked a lot like your backyard.

"Hey, buddy. Watcha doin'?"

The voice caught me by surprise. I spun and saw a future version of you standing on the back deck. A man who shared your bright blue eyes and curly tangle of hair.

"Hi, Dad!" You waved a filthy hand. "We just dug a tunnel to the other side of the earth."

"Really?"

For some reason, he sounded like he didn't believe you.

Following his gaze, I realized why. All of a sudden, our incredibly deep tunnel didn't look so deep after all.

It was just a small hole in the grass.

So *that's* why the other side of the earth looked so much like your backyard. Because it *was* your backyard.

The tunnel was never really there. It was a lot like me.

Imaginary.

4.

Later that same day, Ryan's mom had called him back home, but you and I were still in the backyard. We'd abandoned our tunnel and moved on to more important things.

First, we fought a horde of zombies.

Then we hunted for treasure under the trampoline.

Our work was interrupted when a T. rex came barreling through the fence.

The two of us ran away screaming. Being your imaginary friend was dangerous!

Your parents were on the deck. They didn't seem too worried about the dinosaur attack. Your mom was sitting in the shade, reading a book. Your dad was seated at the wooden table. He'd covered the table with newspaper. About a dozen plastic toys were scattered across the pages. They were small, about the size of his thumb. Fantasy characters. A dragon, a troll, an elf.

A tiny paintbrush was in your dad's hand. He dipped the brush into a bottle of paint and carefully applied it to one of the toys.

When I noticed this, I stopped running. So did you.

And so did the T. rex.

All three of us were distracted by your dad.

"Why's he painting your toys?" I asked.

"They're not my toys," you said. "They're *his*."

The T. rex let out a surprised growl. He hadn't been expecting this. Neither had I.

"I thought only kids played with toys," I said.

The dinosaur nodded in agreement.

"He doesn't really *play* with them," you explained. "He just paints them. Then he puts them on a shelf so he can look at them."

This just kept getting stranger. "Why have toys if you're not gonna play with them?"

You thought about this for a moment, then called out across the yard. "Hey, Dad?"

Your dad looked up. "Yeah?"

"Shovel wants to ask you a question."

He blinked. "Shovel?"

You pointed to me. "My new friend!"

"Oh!" Your dad nodded. "*That* Shovel."

"He wants to know why you have toys if you aren't gonna play with them."

Your mom lowered her book, revealing a grin. "Because your father's a nerd."

Your dad set down the paintbrush. "These aren't *toys*. They're custom-made miniatures."

"Like I said." Your mom winked at you. "*Nerd.*"

"What're they for?" I asked.

"What're they for?" you asked.

Your dad explained. He sometimes got together with friends for something called Dungeons & Dragons. Which involved making up stories about characters that don't exist doing things that never actually happened. They had to roll dice and keep up with character sheets, and the whole thing sounded really complicated.

As he described all this, surprise settled over me. I didn't know grown-ups *also* played pretend!

You approached the table. The T. rex and I followed. As we got closer, I gained a better view of the toy—sorry, *miniature*—your dad was working on. A knight with glittering silver armor. A shield was strapped to his back. The visor of his helmet was raised, showing a very serious face underneath.

There was only one part of the knight that still needed to be painted. His sword.

"Tell you what," your dad said. "Why don't you paint that part?"

You raised your eyebrows. "Really?"

He nodded and you took a seat beside him.

"What color should the sword be?" you asked.

"That's up to you."

You thought for a second. "It should be green."

Green?

I'd only existed for a few hours, but I already knew: Swords aren't green. But you weren't letting that stop you.

"See…um…the knight stuck his sword into a swamp," you explained. "A magical swamp. And that turned his sword green."

"Oh! It's a swamp-sword."

"Yeah!"

I looked from you to your dad. I could see where you got your imagination from.

With a little help from your parents, you carefully painted the knight's sword a swampy green.

"Nice work, kiddo!" Your mom tousled your hair.

"That's the awesomest swamp-sword I've ever seen!" your dad said.

He held up his hand and you high-fived it.

You were smiling.

So was he.

You both had those same eyes, that same tangle of hair.

It's one of my favorite memories.

And one of my saddest.

Because I know what's going to happen next.

The story continues in

IMAGINARY

LEE BACON is the author of several books for young people, including *The Last Human* and the Joshua Dread and Legendtopia series, as well as the original audio story *The Mystery of Alice*. His books have been translated into twenty-three languages. Lee grew up in Texas and now lives in New Jersey.